1.

Where trees conceal and waters meet,
The one shall bring you what you seek.
Where dead wood trees to heavens reach,
Shall be the place where two worlds meet

Where day breaks to darkest night,
Evil feeds like a parasite
Where children bleed beneath the tree,
The kingdom of the damned shall be

The river Staple began high up in the cold mountains of the North where the fresh snow that covered their peaks would melt quietly upon the gentle touch of the mid morning sun. Undisturbed and unnoticed, the droplets would form and fall from the snowy overhangs which capped the mountain peaks. Who would believe that this great river could have such quiet and humble beginnings but, as with many things, the blueprint for what it was to become could be seen there right at it's conception. The droplets of water cut thin veins through the mountain snow on their descent, in time the snow would give way to rocks and fields, boulders and steep canyons but in the mountains of the North the river was young and delicate, it would dance its way gently down the rocks, full of potential and longing. It flowed with the ease of a child that takes such great delight in the new world it has found itself in, a world of mystery and magic and wonder. Follow your own river back to its source, let it lead you back to that magic and wonderful world you were born into, to a world full of questions that needed few answers. Bathe in those cold, crisp early waters and follow them as they carry you down the mountain. Look at the first little flowers that have somehow made their way into the small cracks of the rock and bravely reach out into the biting wind. The bright, elegant colours of their wind beaten faces reflect in the water as the stream flows on. Watch as the eagle settles onto the rock and washes its wings in the crystal clear water. Feel the chill as the water flows into the shadows of these great mountains and gets funnelled through the steep rocky canyons, gently smoothing the surfaces beneath with its tender and relentless touch. The river is beginning to grow, to develop and it carves through the valley like a lost highway.

The mountains climb so high that the peaks burst through the clouds and into the heavens above; they cast enormous shadows that cover the land in a thick, dark blanket. The river rages through the rocks and rumbles down the waterfalls, the sounds bouncing off the mountain walls creating an eerie echo, it's as if the mountains themselves are speaking through the very river they created. As the river flows further into the shadows the highest mountains fall behind and fill the horizon. When the river finally breaks free from the darkness and bursts through into the bright sunlight you can almost hear it singing a joyful 'Hallelu-iah'.

The water is so pure that at night the moonlight bounces off it and lights up the land like a strip-light in a darkened room. It travels the entire length of this great land on its journey to the sea. At some points it is violent and fierce, leaving all who bear witness forever humbled by its force. At other points it is slow and gentle, the surrounding land imbued with a deep sense of peace and wonder. The river represents every man; woman and child born to the soil it dissects and they in turn carry a little piece of it wherever they wander.

I could devote this entire book to the course of the river. Its journey takes it through some of the most beautiful countryside that it is possible to imagine. It passes through rolling hills, thick forest, ravines with their steep, red rock face climbing high into the heavens. It crashes down waterfalls, slides lazily round long turns. It moves through villages as fishermen sit out in the sun on her banks with expectant rod in hand. Children splash and play in the water, Swans lead their young, Otters build their dams and countless different animals have their homes nestled in safely besides her. So much life, so completely dependent on those warm, mid morning rays which quietly melt the snow-capped peaks of the North. As with all things in the world of man it was at some point given a name. Who named her and why will forever be lost to the curves of her timeline but as far as we know the name has always remained the same. She is called the River Staple and it is beside her banks that our young hero has a chance encounter with fate, although how much fate is ever left to chance we will never know. At the very place where the young boy's fate entwines with that of the strange and mysterious old man, a black bird now sits with narrow eyes sparkling in the light of the round moon. In one graceful movement he lifts from the ground, leaving the banks behind and flies high into the night sky. His strong wings beat the air beneath them and he soars higher and higher until the river is lost in the darkness beneath. It is a still night, eerily quiet - as the black bird catches a current, arcs and turns, there is barely a sound from the thick forest below. With the smallest movement he flicks his wings and lets the warm current that rises from the woodland lift him high up in the air. With wings stretched out besides him he glides effortlessly through the cold night. The forest covers the countryside for miles, the treetops dominate the horizon for almost as far as the eye can see but in the distance he can make out a warm orange glow. He beats the air hard again, eager to reach the distant light that promises of warmth and comfort. As he glides closer he can see that the forest eventually comes to an abrupt halt, like a full stop at the end of a sentence. The forest is gone and at its edge sits a small village surrounded by well-worked fields. The moonlight reflects off the glass windows of the small wooden cabins and the faint glow of firelight can be seen within. The air is so still that the smoke from the chimneys drifts straight up into the sky above. The soft, orange glow that could be seen all those miles away is coming from a building that sits in the middle of the village. It is by far the largest with three bright lanterns hanging from the porch and a high pointed wooden roof. As the black bird makes his descent towards the porch he can hear the faint chatter of people coming from inside. Large wooden steps lead up to the porch and the big, sturdy door is flanked by two huge glass windows; each tapering to a sharp peak like the roof above. He glides down and, with just a couple of flaps of his wings comes to rest gracefully on the beam beneath the porch. He edges his way along and settles close to the middle lantern where he sits comfortably and bathes in the warmth of the flame.

2.

There was something different tonight. Something different in the candlelight, which was normally so soft and warm. The eight little flames that had danced so joyfully in the light mid-summer breeze flicked backwards and forwards with nervous agitation, casting sinister shadows across the wooden walls.

The lined faces of the village elders, usually so serene, seemed strained and anxious as if their features betrayed an unspoken fear that they longed to remain hidden. A sense of unease quickly worked its way through the rest of the gathering. Luke Shears sat perfectly still as the rest of the villagers' nervous chatter grew until it blended into one loud, sharp noise that filled the hall and spilled out into the evening air. He slowly raised a rough, well-worked hand and stroked the blonde beard that hung comfortably from his face. As he did it would show just the smallest hint of grey beneath; this was a movement that his children knew well and he would often sit beside the warm fire quietly stroking his beard, watching flames lick around a well seasoned log. Just as the noise was reaching fever pitch a hammer came down hard on the huge table.

'Quiet please…quiet now, settle down', his voice had a deep gravely bass that almost shook the foundations of the building. Jacob Batterby had the most incredible voice. He never had to shout and yet he never struggled to be heard. It was almost as if the very tone of his words resonated perfectly with the waters of the human body. His voice was felt as much as heard and as such it was imbued with a strange authority, wisdom and power.

Jacob stood up to his full six feet six. Even the weight of all the years he carried couldn't prevent him from standing straight and tall. His large, weathered hand clung to the hammer and the other, outstretched, gestured to those seated around the table. He looked each of the 14 men straight in the eye with thick, grey sideburns framing his proud face.

The room silenced instantly and the people began to shuffle anxiously in their chairs.

Passing travellers, merchants and shepherds had brought with them stories. Terrible stories, horrors of which had never been heard before in this quiet village. They told of foul misshapen creatures which carried the stench of death with them. A smell so vile it could travel for miles on the lightest breeze. The smell oozed from their pestilent, wart covered skin. Their long faces fell like dripping wax to a sharp pointed chin. With skin so pale that no blood could be running through their veins. Mouths full of sharp, cracked, dirty teeth and a thin tongue which slipped in and out greedily like a snake tasting the air. A huge nose hung down almost to their chin and…their hands….Each long, bony finger was the length of a man's fore arm with dirty talons for nails. These long, wiry fingers stretched out from thin skeletal arms and it was said that they could crush a man's head in those very hands.

They told of these creatures hovering silently into far away villages at night covered in dark, hooded capes. As cold and quiet as death itself they would peer through windows while the people slept unaware. Sniffing the air with their long, hooked noses, tasting it with silvery tongues.….reaching in with their bony fingers, desperately searching, sniffing and clawing around for a small child. Before the children had a chance to scream their hands would be on them. Wrapping their way over their mouths, stifling any sound they tried to make and silently they would be pulled out into the night, never to be seen again. In the morning parents would wake to a silent house and empty beds. Nothing but that deathly stench left in their place. That was why they had all gathered here so anxiously tonight, each one of them longing to find comfort in Jacob's words.

'We all know why we are here tonight', he said slowly and calmly. 'Many a man has brought with him tales of these creatures, these snatchers as they are being called. Never in my 85 years have I heard of such atrocities. They may well just be stories passed from man to man becoming more poisonous at every pass. As of yet there has been no evidence of these creatures' existence but the reports of children going missing are true. Taken from their very beds as they sleep and I would rather believe that this was the work of these 'Snatchers' (he almost hissed the word), 'than the work of our fellow man'. A thick silence filled the room. The men had not found the solace they had so desperately come to seek. The eyes of the elders said it all. In none of the young men's short lives had they seen them so troubled.

The candlelight was casting some strange shadows that night and the people gathering couldn't help but glance nervously around the room. Each one almost expecting to see the clawed hand of a snatcher reaching out for them from the darkness that lay behind. Luke sat listening intently with his strong, rough hands now clasped together, thumbs moving against each other in a slow, circular automatic movement. Even his grey-specked beard failed to disguise the horror he was feeling at the thought of one of these devilish creatures getting anywhere near his three precious children. He thought of them at home already tucked up in bed and had to fight the urge not to just get up and run to their side. His hands briefly clenched into tight fists as he thought of those long bony fingers reaching in through their window. There was no doubt that he would fight those creatures, those snatchers, with every last breath in his body if he had to. He let out a deep breath and relaxed as once more Jacob's rich voice filled the room.

"The tales have reached us from travellers coming from the south and the east. There are grieving villages living in fear, their children too scared to sleep. Well, we will not let ourselves become corrupted by this fear, we must remain strong, vigilant and ready for the sakes of our children'.

Jacob's voice grew louder and he lent forwards, resting both hands on the solid wooden table in front of him, his steady gaze locking eyes with the individual men.

'It is now the turn for whoever or whatever is committing these acts to feel afraid for if they dare to breach the boundaries of this village then we will be ready and they will be punished'.

He had practically roared the last few words and the hall erupted. It felt as if the very walls were shaking from the sheer force of that powerful voice and the men stood cheering, fists raised in the air, their fear briefly replaced by a new-found strength and resolve.

Even in times as terrible as these Luke found it hard not to admire Jacob Batterby's timing. Each world delivered perfectly to give the maximum effect.

3.

The windows rattled quietly within their frames and the children were sitting upright on their beds. The candle had long since burnt down and there was nothing to light the room except the moonlight, which made its way through the thin net curtains.

'I've heard that they boil the children and then eat them bit by bit. That they carry the boiled heads on their backs, that's why they smell so horrible...it's the smell of dead children's boiled heads'. Julie was only six and she began to cry as the words came out of her mouth. Wendy left the warm sheet that had been pulled right up to her chin and moved over to her little sister's bed to comfort her. Julie had only ever known long, warm summers spent out playing games in the fields or helping her mother tend to the vegetable patch. Or cold, crisp winters spent besides a crackling fire. All this talk of snatchers with their long bony, clawed hands was too horrible to even imagine.

'Don't be silly', said James. 'There's no such thing as snatchers. It's just stories the travellers make up so they can get a hot meal and a warm bed to sleep in on their way through.' James was only twelve and he was trying so hard to sound brave but every time the glass rattled or the curtains moved his heart would flutter and his eyes would dart nervously to the window behind them.

'But why would they say that? Why would they try to scare us?

They've never done it before. They used to tell us about the huge boats that would land on the beach and the strange fruits and gem stones the men would bring with them. Or of the small people that live in the caves to the west who drink a magic drink that makes them sing and dance all night. Why are they telling stories about snatchers and missing children? I don't want to hear those horrible stories'. A little tear fell down her cheek and he wished he could answer her question and make them all feel better but he couldn't. Soon his dad would be back from the meeting at the hall and quietly slide his smiling face round the door to wish them good night. Then they'd all be safe because he wouldn't let any snatchers get them. He was the strongest man in the whole village and if there were such a thing then he could kill ten or twenty snatchers with his bare hands, he was sure of that. But for now the moonlight was barely bright enough for them to make each other out and their imagination was beginning to play tricks on them.

The children had never really had anything to fear before. They'd heard the stories about the great battles which had been fought when Jacob Batterby had been a boy and they were all scared of Mr. Forthright the local teacher when he went all red in the face and angry. But they had never been scared of the dark before this evening.

James couldn't sleep, his mind was too full of thoughts and he couldn't make sense of any of it. The whole day had felt like a dream; the strange old man, his shaggy dog and weird words that made no sense and that…. Then suddenly he laughed quietly to himself, it was a dream, it must've been a dream, he probably just fell asleep without knowing it. As he rolled over to go back to sleep he felt a pain in the top of his thigh where he had turned onto something hard that lay in his pocket. It felt as though his heart missed a beat, it was real, he hadn't been dreaming. Quickly he reached down into his pyjama pocket and sure enough there it was. He felt the cool, smooth curve in the palm of his hand, the smoothest thing he'd ever felt in his life. It was as if all his busy thoughts had suddenly cleared and his mind felt like a freshly tidied room. He held the soft, round object tight, it was so smooth that he worried it could slip from his grasp at any moment. But the tighter he squeezed it the harder it would become. 'That's strange', he thought and he loosened his grip until it became soft and tender. He gently rubbed the smooth surface with his thumb and if he pressed ever so lightly then he could feel it bend and give way. He squeezed hard suddenly and it became like granite, even harder than granite maybe? he imagined it to be the hardest thing in the world. He longed to pull it out from underneath the covers and gaze at it but he had to keep it hidden because it would sparkle like a star in the moonlight. He felt the shiver of electricity that ran up his spine every time he touched it and lay there safe in the knowledge that it hadn't all been a dream. After all, he had the proof right there in his pyjama pocket. Suddenly he felt very alone, ashamed and frightened. It seemed tonight was to be the first of many things because he had never kept a secret from his beloved sisters before either.

4.

Bugatti made his way to the end of the forest track and into the field that waited. The forest floor had been painted in a patchwork of quivering light where the sun had broken through the thick leaves above. The dense forest gave way to a large, unkempt field full of thick, long grass and wild flowers. The warm sun caressed his face and the grass brushed through his fingers. Behind followed his ever-faithful companion Dowser, the long, shaggy haired dog who had followed him so lovingly all these years.

Bees and insects flew from flower to flower and the grass swayed like the rise and fall of a gentle tide. It had been a long time since they'd both ventured back to Maya woods and he hadn't realised just how much he'd missed them.

He knew that the riverbank lay just half a mile further and that the brook was one of the most beautiful places in the whole of the world where a man could quench his thirst. He took it all in as he headed closer to the river, breathing in those summer smells that only someone who has spent the season in the unspoilt countryside could fully appreciate. The field was long and wide but surrounded on three sides by the forest. He made his way through the field in big long strides with his grey beard almost tickling the top of the grass and watched as Dowser ran, his dark head only just rising from the surface. The sun had begun its slow descent back into the earth but its rays were all the more pleasant for it. It had been a strange instinct that had brought him all these miles, a nagging sense that he couldn't ignore. For months his dreams had been bringing him to this very field, he had not been here since he was a boy but the images were still crisp in his mind. He almost felt as though he was coming home, a feeling he hadn't felt for a long time. Bugatti's whole life had been guided by instinct, he had searched for the Wayli flower for more years that he could even remember. It had been twenty five years now since he had last found one, a quarter of a century and he began to fear he might never see one again. His time must be nearing its end he often thought to himself but age had taught him many things, one of them being that the journey is the true treasure, not the find itself. He knew only too well the virtue of patience but still he found himself, thinking that if there could never be a more perfect place to find the mysterious and elusive flower than here, by the banks of the river Staple.

5.

The following morning began much the same way as every other summer's morning in the village. The roosters crowed and the birds sang to rejoice in the start of a new day.

The three children awoke, bleary eyed after a restless night's sleep. James's dreams had been particularly vivid. Even as he awoke he found it hard to untangle himself from their strange and terrifying imagery. He had dreamt of a forest. It was the daytime but black as the darkest night. The trees that surrounded him were so tall that he imagined you could probably climb right up into the clouds. All the trees were dead and there was an eerie silence. No birds resting on the dead branches, no animals rustling in the undergrowth. Nothing but the sound of his breath and his own heart beating. It was too dark to make out much detail but the trees towered above and it began to feel as if they were closing in on him. His heart began to beat faster and faster and he felt as if he was being watched, stalked by some unseen hunter. He didn't know which way to go but he knew he must run. Try to find a way out this suffocating, black forest. The fear had overcome him and he ran as fast as he could manage, hands out in front of him but dead branches and bushes were ripping at his skin and his face. He could feel blood slowly making its way down his forehead and into his eyes but he didn't want to stop. He didn't know what he was running from but he knew that it was getting closer. Then suddenly he came to a small opening and he stopped to look up. He had to strain his eyes to see but in the middle was the tallest, most terrifying tree he'd ever seen. It stretched up high into the heavens above. Its dead branches hung out from its vast black trunk. Dead roots spread out before him like a spider's web. He felt an unearthly cold chill tickle its way up his spine. He looked up at the tree in absolute terror and it looked down on him like a man to an ant. It was so dark that he hadn't even noticed as the roots began to snake their way silently closer and closer towards his feet. He started to walk slowly around the edge of the tree, as quietly as he could. He didn't know why he was trying to be so quiet but it was as if he didn't want to wake the dead tree itself. He knew that there was something evil about that tree and he could feel its cold glare bearing down on him. Suddenly he realised that the ground had become sticky. As if he was walking through clay. He stopped and looked hard into the dark beneath him. It took a while for his eyes to adjust and just as he realised that the earth was soaked in blood he felt the tight squeeze around his ankle. He let out a scream so loud that his whole body shook with the sound but the darkness swallowed it up. He tried to turn and twist his way out of the grip but it was too strong and a root had taken hold of his other ankle now, like snakes he felt them wrapping their way around him faster and faster until they were up to his chest. They were squeezing harder, forcing every last bit of air from his lungs. There was none left even to scream. Now they were up around his neck, wrapping around and around and then they pulled. So fast and so hard dragging him deep into the bloodied ground beneath.....

'Are you OK, darling?' James shivered back to his senses. 'Look at you, you're trembling like a leaf, come here.' This time it was his mother who wrapped him up in her warm arms. 'It's all those stories the kids have been telling you isn't it....about them snatchers? I don't know where people dream stuff like that up, horrible things to tell the children. Now don't you worry, nothing like that's going happen around here. The worst thing you'll have to deal with is Mr. Forthright's temper if you're late. Now best you run along, we all know nothing annoys him more!'

The three children rushed out to the paddock where their father was feeding the horses. Luke Shears was the village metal worker. His hands had grown tough and hard from years of working the hot metal. He had bushy fair hair, a thick blonde beard and a smile that sometimes seemed almost as broad as his shoulders. His eyes were full of love at the best of times but never more so than when his three children rushed up to kiss him goodbye. Well two of them!...James was getting a bit old for that now and every morning Luke had to fight hard to stop himself. He knew that James had outgrown that and was fast becoming a man. Fortunately both Wendy and Julie had shown no signs of wanting it to stop.

He reached down and picked them both up, one in each strong arm.

'Right girls, be good today, don't you go giving dear old Mr. Forthright a hard time', he said giving them each a wink. They both knew that he secretly took great delight in watching uptight Mr. Forthright working himself up into a frenzy! He set the two girls back on their feet.

'Aren't you going to say 'bye to Meg?', he asked patting the little old grey horse that stood eating the hay behind him. They both give Meg a quick stroke and then headed of down the path.

'And you son', he said ruffling the top of James's head with big, heavy hands. 'You enjoy yourself, that's what school's for!' He flashed him another big, broad grin and then turned back to Meg.

James stood there for a while desperately wanting to tell his dad what he'd found. He reached into his pocket once more and felt it softly rubbing against his palm but then reluctantly he turned and followed his sisters up the path. The old man's words were still running around his head.

'What you will find is for you and for you only. No one else must ever be allowed to lay their hands upon it. Only you will know what it's for and what to do with it. If it is ever to fall into the wrong hands then all this is lost. When the time comes you must be willing to make the sacrifice, the fate of the worlds depends on it'.

6.

Bugatti had slept restlessly, his dreams vivid and untamed. The embers of the fire were still smoking from the night before and he was thirsty. He reached down to fill his flask; the water that comes trickling down the brook and into the river is crystal clear. He took a great big sip and the water almost tasted sweet. After he'd drunk as much as he needed he sat back down on the riverbank with the morning sun on his face and Dowser came to rest his head comfortably on his lap. Bugatti had spent the entire afternoon before searching every inch of the field, he was sure nothing had been missed. His keen eyes had travelled down the riverbanks and into the surrounding woodland. He couldn't help but feel a slight disappointment. It was his own fault he thought to himself, he didn't want to admit it but there had been a part of him that was certain he would find that delicate little flower resting beside the brook. There was something else troubling him too, he sensed a presence he had not felt since way back to a time that he had hoped to forget. Maybe it was just being back here after all these years that had stirred up so many old memories. Had his intuition really grown so weak that he could no longer trust it, or perhaps it was being clouded by his feelings? He couldn't tell. They both sat together silently, Bugatti deep in thought and Dowser letting out long, slow breaths as he slept on his lap.

'He must be tired', he thought as he looked down at his old friend. It had been a long journey and neither of them were as young as they used to be. His quests for the Wayli flower had taken them to some amazing, far off lands. Through ice glaciers and long, hot deserts; to snow-topped mountains and valleys which not so long ago lay at the bottom of a great ocean. Through all of it Dowser had been his constant companion, with his shaggy black and white hair and smiling eyes, Bugatti could think of no-one better to have shared it with. He gently ran his fingers through the shaggy coat and let his mind carry him far away. He was in an unusually nostalgic mood, his mind had taken him back to a time so long ago that the many memories had blended together like paint on an artist's palette and all that was left was a feeling. For, like the memories both the feelings of love and sadness, joy and regret had also merged together into an emotion so complex and all encompassing that he had little choice but to let its tide wash over him. Even after all these years in many ways the human heart remained such a mystery to the old man but he knew better than to ignore it. Suddenly he was pulled from his nostalgic reverie as Dowser sprang to his feet, eyes alert and nose lifted high in the air picking up on a hidden scent too subtle even for Bugatti's acute senses. Sure enough, there it was, impossibly faint but there none the less. The distant sound of movement, leaves being brushed aside and soil crunching under foot. It was still a long way off and no normal man would have been able to detect it but Bugatti was no ordinary man. Dowser's fine nose had saved his life on more than one occasion so he quietened his mind and placed the palm of his hands delicately on the ground. From the subtle vibrations of the earth he could tell that someone or something was running, the footsteps came in two's so it couldn't be an animal, they were light, too light to be those of a man, it was a child. He relaxed in an instant. He had learned to become wary of men over the years. He was not afraid of them but the men themselves tended to fear what they did not understand. Fear can lead a man to do a great many terrible things, most of which he had witnessed....most of which.

After several minutes had passed he looked up towards the

sound and, sure enough, over in the far corner of the field a small fair-haired boy had come bursting out of the woodland. He was too far away to be able to see the old man and the dog and ran through the long grass with all the abandon of someone who believes no-one else is watching.

He reached down to fill his flask for the young boy who must be coming for a drink. 'It's a couple of hours walk from the nearest village to this hidden field and if he's been running like that he's probably built up quite a thirst', the old man thought to himself.

The boy was getting closer and had obviously just spotted his unexpected company. His run quickly slowed to a walk and he stared with his big brown eyes, unsure what to make of the old man in the distance. Bugatti knew that he could cut quite an imposing figure, especially to a child so he smiled and beckoned the boy over. The boy approached cautiously, Dowser trotted over to him, tail wagging, forcing his nose up into the boy's hand and he looked immediately more relaxed. Bugatti looked up to greet the fair-haired boy who was now only a couple of hundred metres away and as he did his heart nearly stopped beating. It can't be. He looked again but even at this distance there was clearly no mistaking it.

He had spent much of his life scanning vast horizons for that smallest of flowers with the distinctive red and black petals and the pattern so beautiful it can scarcely be described. There, sure enough, held delicately between the boy's fingers was the Wayli flower. Twenty five years he has been searching and……….and then it hits him. For an instant the world stopped, Bugatti could only describe that moment as being comparable to his own birth or death. For in many ways it was both.

The very first thing his master had ever taught him had been that rhyme. He had made him recite it with every meal and had constantly told him that of all the things he could ever teach that rhyme was the one thing he must always remember. He had long since given up on his magical training. It had brought him nothing but heartache and suffering but to this day he still repeated those words with every meal. His intuition had always been strong but he had never been able to understand the cryptic words. He had begun to wonder whether it had all just been a trick or a strange lesson from his master. Centuries had passed and he knew the rhyme as well as he knew his own name. All those long years and it's only now as the boy approaches that it begins to make sense.

Bugatti turned once more to the brook and the river and closed his eyes. He let the warm sun soothe his skin and then he said goodbye for he knew that from this day forth things would never be the same again. As he turned back to face the boy there was only one thing going through his mind.

> 'Where trees conceal and waters meet,
> The one shall bring you what you seek
> Where dead wood trees to heavens reach,
> Shall be the place where two worlds meet'

7.

'It's been found…..it's been found', she screamed over and over again. Her words echoed and rattled around the dark cavern until it sounded like an army of frenzied witches all shrieking the same chant.

The snatchers had been working hard, digging further and deeper into the earth. Her piercing screams filled all four caverns. Many centuries had passed and Zelda had waited impatiently throughout them all for this day to come. She was still weak and still trapped in her earthy tomb but her powers were returning slowly and her body was starting to form. It had been a long time since she'd felt blood running through her veins or heard the sound of her beating heart. She lay as she had done for all those years, trapped unable to move; a disgusting mixture of wooden roots and human flesh. Where her hands and feet should be there were roots which led deep into the earth below. Where the body had begun to form the skin was so thin and pale that you could see straight through it, it was so transparent that you could trace every vein. She was already starting to show that bewitching beauty she'd possessed centuries ago. Her face was framed with long, jet black hair and it spread out on the dirt beneath her. Her powers would soon be strong enough to find the sphere. For now though her gaze was blurred and unsteady. Each snatcher she drew from the blackness of her soul and forged with the earth around her had left her weakened and the wooden prison would reclaim a little more of her tortured body. The unfortunate soul who had discovered the sphere still had a little while left to live.

She gazed up at the same dark sodden earth roof she had been watching for centuries upon centuries, her spirit growing more twisted with every torturous day that passed.

The snatchers came crawling over to her side, hissing with delight. These creatures gave her only the briefest respite from the cruel centuries she had endured. They were her children, born from an imagination that had been twisted with pain and polluted by the need for revenge. Creatures this terrifyingly foul could have come from no other and she gazed at them like a proud mother. The blood of every child that they had ripped silently from their sleep was the blood of hope and she tasted it as it seeped slowly through the soil and into the hungry roots below. She knew of the powers that the legendary sphere possessed and she longed for it with every evil fibre in her body. With the sphere she could once more freely roam and rule her black earth. She could return the suffering ten fold on the race that had delivered her to this fate. That had created a monster like no other and she in turn would create an army of them, an army built from the nightmares they couldn't yet imagine.

'It's been found', she screamed again and once again the snatchers hissed their delight. 'I need my strength if I'm to find it. Now bring me blood, BRING ME BLOOD', she shrieked. The snatchers knew exactly what to do and before the echoes had made their final call they were already crawling out of the small crack which led back to the dark earth above.

8.

James approached the old man with the piercing eyes and his dog slowly. He was surprisingly tall, his clothes were tatty and torn but they flowed from his body with an almost regal elegance. He looked like a great explorer returning home from a long, noble expedition. You could almost see the stories which lay in the lines of his face and that hung from his dirty grey beard. The closer James got the taller the man seemed to become and his heart began to beat just a little faster as he sensed something slightly dangerous in the man ahead. His dark eyes shone with a depth that he hadn't seen before. He had no doubt that they could quickly turn into the most terrifying stare but for now they were warm and welcoming.

The black and white shaggy haired dog came over to greet him first. It thrust its warm nose up into his free hand and wagged its tail playfully.

'That's a rather beautiful flower your holding'. The voice was exactly as he had imagined. It was rich and warm with an underlying fierceness that almost seemed to tie all the warm tones together. He'd totally forgotten about the tiny red and black flower he'd been holding between his fingers.

'Oh this....I've never seen one of these before.' He didn't know why his voice shook but the more he gazed at the old man the smaller and younger he began to feel. 'I found this back there in the woods. My mother loves her flowers and I don't think even she will have seen one like this before so I picked it for her. It was very strange though. It didn't even have a root, it was almost as if it had been balancing on top of the soil just waiting for someone to come and pick it'. He relaxed a little a felt that he wasn't in any danger, the stranger's eyes and warm smile had told him this but for some reason his heart was beating fast and the words flew nervously from his lips. 'Do you know anything about this flower?'

'I believe there is no one walking this earth who knows more', the old man smiled and James believed him. 'There's much to tell you about but for now have a drink, James, you must be thirsty.' He held out his flask and it took him a couple of sips before he realised, startled that the old man had known his name.

'How do you know my name?' the boy asked, feeling anxious and unsettled again.

'You told me.'

James quickly replayed the conversation in his head and knew for certain that he hadn't mentioned it.

'You've told me a great many things, perhaps without knowing you've done so', Bugatti continued, 'just as you already know a great deal about me. Trust your intuition and what it is telling you, my little friend, and you won't go far wrong. We must set about drying this little flower immediately.'

Bugatti held out his hand and James handed it over without even questioning.

It had been twenty five years since he'd held this flower and had to the chance to marvel at its beauty. He studied the intricacy of the pattern and a deep sorrow filled his heart. He knew that this would be the last flower he would find and that his quest for the Wayli plant had finally come to an end. More importantly he knew that the many years he had walked this wondrous planet were drawing to a close and that the few years left would be the hardest and most important he would ever endure.

James watched in absolute fascination and wonder as the old man set about drying the plant. He was as old as Jacob Batterby without a doubt yet every movement was so quick and agile and every muscle so strong. He picked up a large rock effortlessly with one hand and placed it so that the angled side pointed directly at the sun. He delicately set the flower in the middle. He was so careful not to damage the petals and stem. It was as if the flower was the most valuable and precious thing on this entire earth. He leant forwards, blew slowly onto the flower from the bottom of the stem to the very top petal. He repeated this a couple of times and then he closed his eyes and held his hands over the flower almost touching but not quite. Finally he slowly brought his hands together and pulled them into his chest where he held them in the form of a cross before letting out a long deep breath, releasing and opening his eyes once more.

'Sit with me on this bank, there is much we should talk about. First, allow me to introduce myself. My name is Bugatti and this here is Dowser, the greatest friend a man could have.' James looked down at Dowser's happy face and ran his fingers through the dog's shaggy hair.

'So what brings you here to this magical place?' Bugatti asked.

The sun was shining down on the back of his head and the sound of running water left him feeling warmed and contented; his heart had finally settled down and he felt strangely comfortable in the presence of the man and his dog.

'I often come here', he said. 'I like to sit on this bank and listen to the sound of the brook running into the river. I like to imagine all the different places the river must run through on its journey to the sea. I've never seen the sea and I dream about all the boats and sailors with all their treasures and stories to tell.'

James had almost got lost in his own little world and Bugatti sat there eager to listen.

'I like to imagine making my way to the beaches and boats and travelling the seas, finding new lands and adventures'.

'So, the wandering spirit, the spirit of adventure lies inside you then, James. Good.' He almost smirked. 'I have a feeling you are going to need it.'

'So are you a magician?', James asked, almost embarrassed in case he would make fun of his childish imagination.

'Your intuition serves you well', Bugatti laughed. 'Well, I used to be a magician but I haven't practiced much of the art for a good many years now, only what I need to get by.' He smiled. 'Magic is a dangerous thing and I have seen many a great man and woman seduced by the powers it can hold. I am in fact the last in a long line of people to have been trained in the ways of the magi.'

The old man turned away and James could sense a hint of sadness in his voice.

'Against my teachers wishes I have decided to let the art die out with these old bones so I'm afraid that I will be the first and last magician you will ever meet! I'm not completely useless though, I still have a certain amount of mastery over the five elements although…..'

'Five elements?....I thought there were only four', James interrupted, thinking back to one of Mr. Forthright's lessons under the apple tree.

'Of course not.'

His tone was firm and James suddenly began to worry that he'd angered the strange old man. 'The fifth element is the most important of all. Without it the others could never exist'.

James could tell that he had much to say so he sat there quietly urging him to go on.

'You must remember, my little friend, that of all this which lies before you, all the great adventures and travels you will undertake, there is only one journey that's of any real importance. You must learn to follow the brooks and rivers which are running through these very veins', he said, reaching out to take James's wrist, squeezing until the thin blue veins rose to the surface. 'You must follow the rivers deeper and deeper inside yourself becoming familiar with every place you pass. You must follow the river all the way to the sea of your fifth element, the element which lies within and without this body you know. Only there will you find treasures of any real value. Treasures that shall make your eyes shine and sparkle more brilliant than any diamond you could find out here.' He moved his arm in one long, slowly arced gesture at the land in front of them.

'Four elements', the old man laughed to himself... 'next you'll be telling me there are only five senses', he chuckled again, 'just because they only have five, doesn't mean that you must.'

James sat there silently. He'd never heard words like this before. He felt an inexplicable closeness and wonder for this old man and his dog; they felt familiar to him somehow although he was sure they had never met. As he sat there in the late morning sun he realised that the world had never looked so beautiful and magical in all his twelve years as it did today.

'You will find something today, James.' The old man suddenly looked stern and serious. James gave him the appropriate look to let him know that he was giving his words the due attention. 'What you will find will change the course of your life and possibly all our lives forever.' He sat in absolute wonder and bewilderment but the man went on, 'what you will find is for you and for you only. No one else must ever be allowed to lay their hands upon it. Only you will know what it's for and what to do with it. If it is ever to fall into the wrong hands then all this is lost.' He looked straight into the boy's brown eyes and spoke slowly to make sure each word was heard and understood. 'When the time comes you must be willing to make the sacrifice, not once but twice. The fate of the worlds depends on it.' Bugatti stopped to allow time for the words to settle in James's young mind and then he went on. 'What you will find is both the greatest gift and greatest curse that could be bestowed on a man. You must live and die with it in your hands.'

James couldn't believe what he was hearing and was beginning to wonder if the old man was just completely mad.

'I'm sorry but I don't understand?', he said with a slight waver in his voice. This talk of living and dying with it, whatever it was, in his hands had made him feel uncomfortable and he shuffled nervously but still the old man went on.

'I know this is hard for you to understand now but you must listen and you must remember what I am telling you. This flower you have brought is for me. I have walked this earth for hundreds of years and it has all been leading up to these, my dying days.'

'Hundreds of years!', James exclaimed, now he really was beginning to think that this old man was mad. But still Bugatti went on as if the boy hadn't uttered a word.

'Both of our lives and those of all you know are set to change from this day forth. Yours is a fate that cannot be altered and for one so young I just hope you are ready to rise to the great many challenges which have been set for you.'

James sat there with the words running through his head. He was completely confused.

They sat together in silence and as he ran the words over in his mind he became increasingly doubtful.

'If you're really a magician then can you do something to prove it?', he asked.

Once again he feared that he had angered the man for he turned to face him with a far more severe look this time, it was almost as if he was looking straight through him.

'It is your initial feelings that are to be trusted, James, it doesn't take long for them to become poisoned by thought.' He spat the word 'thought' out with utter contempt.

'Now go, there is no time to waste, I don't know where you will find it but my advice would be to return to the place where you found this magical flower. I can tell you no more for now but rest assured that we shall meet again.'

9.

The snatchers sniffed the air greedily letting the scent guide them from window to window. Under the light of a cold new moon they had crept into the sleeping village. Their pale skin seemed to glow in the equally pale moonlight. They followed each other in absolute silence eager not leave any tracks. The scent had led them to a small wooden house, slightly set apart from the others. Wind chimes hung from the porch above potted plants and their soft sounds sung in the even air.

The window was opened ever so slightly and the snatcher raised her long, hooked nose up to the crack. She let the smell fill her lungs and she could almost taste the little girl who slept inside. Ever so quietly her long fingers began to open the window. Any small creaks where easily covered by the music of the wind chimes. Soon the window was open wide and all three snatchers peered in at the young girl who slept with her teddy gripped tightly in her hands. The girl wasn't any older than eight and she stirred slightly in her sleep as if some part of her sensed the evil eyes watching. But it was too late now. The thin, bony arm was reaching in, fingers outstretched. Reaching closer and closer to the innocent victim. The huge hands looked as though they could wrap all the way around the little girl.

The strike was lightening fast. Before there was any chance to scream, the strong fingers had wrapped their way tightly around her face and over her mouth, suffocating the sound. The poor little girl who couldn't even imagine the horrible fate that awaited her had those festering, stinking, foul hands all over her. Quickly and silently she was eased through the window and pulled out into the cold night air.

10.

There had been a strange atmosphere hanging over the village for the past few weeks. For the children life was continuing pretty much as normal. The weather had been warm and fine and much of their schooling had taken place under the sanctuary of a large apple tree opposite the village hall but even they had begun to notice an unspoken tension that the adults were working so hard to disguise. It was almost impossible for their young minds to understand what had changed, the farmers still tended to their flocks and fields and the women worked hard making costumes for this year's Autumn festival but there was no mistaking it, something just wasn't right. Every smile seemed just a little forced, especially that of Mr. Forthright who seemed to flash it far more often that was suitable or needed. 'Yes, something was very wrong', James thought to himself as he sat under the tree. Mr Forthright was not a tall man, not big, in fact he was quite slight really. His brown moustache seemed to dance on his lip as he spoke and often the words were lost on him, so captivating was that peculiar, hairy dance! But the children knew better than to make fun of him. It wasn't that he was a bad man, just an incredibly bad-tempered man! To be fair to him though he had his work cut out for him, especially on warm sunny says like this when the children just wanted to run and play in the fields.

'BE QUIET, JULIE', Forthright suddenly barked and James

looked over at his little sister at whom the words had been directed. Her head hung slightly and her cheeks were going a little red with embarrassment. As she looked up nervously through her mousey fringe there it was again, a flash of that uneasy and dishonest smile, it seemed to shock the little girl more than any further chastisement ever could. 'Please be quiet, Julie', he went on but in a far gentler tone than normal, 'this is very important'.

'But why's it important?', she asked, 'it's just numbers'.

'Just numbers?', Forthright replied. 'Just numbers', he muttered again quietly under his breath, unable to hide his frustration this time. He flashed another little smile and then went on, 'numbers form the very basis of human thinking, a mastery of numbers represents the very pinnacle of man's intelligence and without them we would simply not be able to function'. He lifted his chin, proud of his bold statement and hoping that it would swiftly silence any who might doubt its importance. But then again that little voice piped up...

'Well I think numbers are silly', Julie said, 'we don't need them at all'. Her face was now flushing as she sat waiting to suffer the full wrath of Forthright's temper.

'Well how then would you propose that we count the sheep in the field?', he asked pointing at the field behind and with a noticeably gruffer delivery.

'That's easy', she replied, 'we just say there are that many', turning to look at the sheep as she spoke.

'That many? How would that ever do? No, no, no. We must always know exactly how many we have of things or how would we know if….if…….if we….lost one of them?', he asked, looking down at the pretty little girl in front.

'Well, we'd give them all names, and then we'd know if any were missing.'

He was now getting increasingly frustrated with the way this discussion was going and his moustache began to twitch with agitation.

'For now, all you need to know about numbers is that you need to know about numbers. Numbers are important because I say they are. Now repeat after me everyone. Two times six is twelve, three times six is eighteen, four times'…..The children all joined in and Forthright found himself celebrating yet another small victory, except that it had left him feeling as unsatisfied as the children he was teaching.

James found his hand reaching into his pocket more and more often. Both his parents had noticed that he was distant and secretly they were beginning to worry about him. He didn't mean to be distant it was just that his thoughts kept taking him back to the river bank and Bugatti's strange words. 'You must live and die with it in your hands'. James was only 12 and he had never even really thought about his own death before that day. He constantly replayed the conversation in his head, eager not to forget any of it. He had remembered vividly what the old man had said about following the brooks and rivers that run through your veins. As often as he could he would go off and find a quiet little spot in the village where he would sit holding the perfect round sphere in his hand. He would try to do as the old man had said and indeed he was slowly changing. He was becoming aware of another part of himself. There was another voice that lay inside his mind. It was not the voice he was used to which would wonder what mum was cooking for supper or got nervous every time he approached Lucy to ask her to go to the festival with him. It ran deeper than this, the old man was right. The words were very faint and unclear but they were there. Holding the sphere brought him a strange but warm feeling of comfort. It was as if it somehow made the world shine just a little brighter. Colours seemed just a little more vivid and patterns more pronounced. It was intoxicating and sometimes he would find himself getting lost in the beauty of the world that surrounded him. It would all be so perfect if it wasn't for that feeling, that sense that he was somehow being watched or hunted, a feeling he couldn't explain but one which left him feeling anxious and uneasy.

Bugatti's instincts had been right. It had taken James a long time to find the spot where he'd picked the flower but as soon as he saw the daffodils growing beside the old, rotten log he recognised it immediately. He searched all around for what must have been an hour. Dusk wasn't far away and he knew that he would have to leave soon if he was to get back before anyone began to worry because it was a long walk from here to the village. He had dug deep into the soil with his bare hands and turned every stone. He longed to find whatever he was meant to find so much. He became angry with the old man for filling his thoughts with those dreams of adventure and slowly became convinced that it had all just been a stupid story. He was angry with himself for having been so drawn in by it all and then just before he was about to give up and go home he kicked out at the log in utter frustration. To his surprise his foot had wedged into the crumbling wood. He pulled it out and it had left a large hole. He thought that seeing as he'd looked everywhere else he may as well have a quick look inside the hole. And there, sure enough, it lay. It was the most beautiful thing he'd ever seen. It was small, just a little bigger than a marble and it shone with a brilliant light. He reached in and the second his fingers touched it an amazing surge of electricity had tingled and sparked its way up his spine. It was an incredible feeling that he couldn't explain, almost as if it made him feel more alive if that was possible. It was so smooth and after he pulled it out he found himself just gazing deeply into it without a thought in his mind. It vaguely resembled a round diamond but inside soft colours of reds, blues, purples and greens seemed to dance and play with each other. It was the strangest consistency. If he touched it gently then it would be soft and malleable but the tighter he squeezed it the harder it would become.

He had spent many hours since that day just holding the sphere and gazing into it. It seemed to grow more beautiful by the day. He felt as if it was somehow becoming a part of him and he couldn't imagine ever not having it with him. Sometimes he almost thought it was trying to speak to him but he would quickly put that down to his imagination. Bugatti had been wrong about one thing, however, he had no idea what it was for or how to use it. But he didn't care, he was just glad that it was his.

Meanwhile Zelda's power was growing stronger with every child the snatchers brought her. Her roots drank the blood hungrily. Her skin was growing thicker and fuller and her face had regained every little bit of beauty it had ever possessed. Already she had one fully formed hand and it was only the other and her feet which kept her rooted to the spot. She was growing more impatient by the day and thought of little else other than holding the sphere in that one, cold hand.

11.

Zelda's gaze had grown steadier and stronger. She knew that it wouldn't be long before she could tell the exact location of the sphere. Already she knew that the finder had been a young boy and that he held the sphere somewhere north-westerly from where she lay. She had also picked up on the presence of someone else, someone she had known from another age. It couldn't be though, she thought to herself, and set about focusing all of her attention on the carrier.

The snatchers were gathered around on the dirt beside her, awaiting their next set of orders. There were now four of them, each one as foul and ugly as the next. She looked up at their long, crooked noses and pitch black eyes that sat in pale skin. She breathed in their foul breath and savoured the sense of pride she felt at having created these monstrosities from the very dirt that held her. She could imagine the sheer terror that the children must feel the first time they set eyes upon them and it brought a sick, tight smile to her lips.

Still though she could not shrug off that familiar presence. She refused to let it lead her back to that time. Those memories had belonged to the body that had died in agony, the body she had been so cruelly forced from. Any love that may have once filled her heart had poisoned and mutated into a vile hatred that had long since corrupted her entire being. The hundreds of years torment that she had endured rooted in the ground had seen to that. All love had turned to hatred and all her thoughts focused only on pain and revenge. She had become drunk on vengeance and her only comfort had been the thought of the suffering she could inflict as soon as she had the power to break free from this insufferable cage. However, since her creation of the snatchers she had managed to find some joy. She had managed to feed that need for vengeance with every young bone that broke in the roots below but it had only given her a taste for more. That was just the start and it would soon be time for the whole of mankind to suffer for the mistakes of their ancestors. She laughed to herself with an evil glee as she realised her long wait was nearly coming to an end.

Night had fallen and the snatchers knew that it was time for them to start their journey from their damp home that was so safely hidden deep in the countryside. It would be days before they reached any form of civilisation. Once again they left her, hissing a farewell as they ran back up the tunnel and out into the awaiting night.

12.

Over the past weeks yet more stories had reached the village. The attacks had been getting more frequent and entire villages had been forced to desert their homes and flee further north. What made matters worse was that no-one seemed to have any idea where the foul creatures came from. They could be moving even closer to their clutches but all they knew was that they could not stay where they were. There was too much hurt, too much fear so they moved, searching for comfort and shelter in the villages that lay beyond.

Luke Shears had been working tirelessly, hammering away on the hot metal, forging it into heavy, razor sharp swords, spears and arrows. He had taken great pains to keep the fruits of his labour away from the eyes of his children and had barely even noticed as the summer swiftly turned to autumn. The nights were indeed shorter and the kids had been missing not having him sat with them beside the fire. He would come in late at night, black with soot and dirt and his hands clearly blistered from working the metal. When the children asked him why he was working so hard he would only tell them that he was doing a very important job for Mr Batterby. The children weren't silly though, they might not know exactly what he was doing but they had a good idea. It seemed that the more effort the adults made to protect the children from their growing fears the more afraid they became. As summer slipped further away the tension within the village grew.

The Autumn Festival celebration was now only a week away. The women had worked hard making the costumes for the parade. It had long been tradition for the village, the parade was meant as a celebration for all that they had harvested from the earth in the summer months and as gratitude for the animals whose meat would sustain them through another long winter. The children would be dressed as lambs and calves and sing and dance around the apple tree, and in the evening there would be a masked ball for the grown ups. Jacob was determined that the celebration would not be affected or overshadowed by this new and unknown threat. No, it was exactly what the village needed after the difficult weeks, a chance to celebrate, to laugh and to forget, if only for one night.

Julie couldn't wait for the festival, she loved getting dressed up and had had so much fun last year. Every night she would rush down to her mum and ask her if she could please try on her little lamb outfit? James and Wendy were both a little older and if anything had begun to feel a bit embarrassed about the dressing up, they felt too grown up for it now even though of course they weren't really! The children and their parents were both just glad that they had something to distract them from the unspoken tension. Jacob was right, it was exactly what the village needed.

The three children perched on the wooden floor close to the fire as their mum sat on a chair putting the final touches to their three outfits. She had always enjoyed sewing. There was something so therapeutic about the way the needle would pop through the animal skin or fabric, with the thread following closely behind. Somehow all these horror stories about snatchers and stolen children had made her love her precious little babies even more, though it scarcely seemed possible. She couldn't help but glance up over her work to watch them playing together on the floor.
'So are you going to kiss Lucy at the dance?!', Wendy asked James teasingly. She knew how embarrassed he got whenever

they brought it up and took great delight in watching his cheeks flush. 'We all know you like her!', she pushed again. Sure enough he began to go all red and coy. Theresa looked up over her sewing with her fingers still working expertly on and couldn't help but laugh.

'Leave the poor boy alone', she said, 'it's you I'm worried about, I've seen the way you look at Peter!'.

'Yeah, you're going to be kissing Peter, eurgh', said little Julie and she pretended to kiss her hand jokingly mimicking the action. They all laughed and James was grateful to have the attention drawn away from him from a while. It gave him a little time for his cheeks to return to their normal colour. Secretly though he had been thinking about his first kiss with Lucy. Well - it would be his first kiss with any girl but he was quietly hoping it would be with Lucy and perhaps the festival would finally provide the opportunity he had been waiting for.

They heard the door close and those familiar heavy steps of their father walking down the corridor towards them. As the door opened Julie ran and jumped up into his arms and he lifted her high up into the air.

'What's going on in here then?'

'It's horrible', said Julie, 'they're all talking about kissing!'. 'Haha, are they now', Luke laughed. 'Well, your mum's the only one I'll be kissing!', he said as he leant down and gave her a great big kiss. His face was covered in dirt and as he stood back up he looked down on his wife and saw that the soot had given her a big black nose.

'Oops, sorry dear!'

The children looked over and all their worries and fears flew away into the night along with the sound of their laughter.

13.

The snatchers crouched over the carcass of a deer on the dirt floor, tearing hungrily at its remains with their teeth and claws. The fresh blood dripping down their chins and covering their bony hands made the skin look even more pale and horrifying. Zelda's power was returning fast, the snatchers had done well and returned with two of the disgusting, whining little creatures this time. One had already been fed to her and the other sat in a small cage made from large animal bones, that lay across the room. The little boy sat with his knees tucked up into his chest and tears rolling down onto them. He cried and begged and it only made her hate him more. She had not shed a single tear for the eternity she had lain there, at least his suffering would be short lived.

Zelda was hungry again and she ordered the snatchers to take the boy from his cage. They were beginning to enjoy this as much as she was, she thought to herself. As they hissed their way across the dirt floor she smiled to herself and wondered what other creatures she would be able to dream up when her power had fully returned. She had possessed a power far greater than any of the others, a power they had been right to fear. The boy looked up in horror as he saw the creatures coming towards him. He forced himself back against the wall, as far as he could possibly go, he was screaming in absolute terror. One of them was lifting up the front of the bony cage and the others stared straight at him with their black, hateful eyes and their snake-like tongues flicking through bloodied teeth. Their stench made him feel physically sick. As their arms reached in to grab him he kicked out frantically, as hard as he could but he was no match for them. Their strong hands were around him again and he cried, begging Zelda for mercy. A snatcher quickly wrapped its hand around his mouth and stifled the sound. As they carried him up the dark tunnel he could hear her laughter filling the cave behind. She was going to enjoy this one.

She felt his life, his energy surging up through the roots and into her body. Yes -, she was stronger now. Her skin was practically glowing and her eyes shone with a beautiful, deranged madness. If she could just quieten her mind then she was sure that she'd be able to track down the carrier. The excitement was almost too much for her, she was so close now. She closed her hand into a tight fist and shut her eyes, she needed to focus. She could feel the pull of the sphere, taking her far to the North West of where she lay. She let it carry her through the hills and valleys. She was so excited that she struggled to maintain focus and the vision would blur and contort. She followed it further, through fields, meadows, villages and then eventually over a river and into a forest. Many of the trees were bare, their leaves had fallen and carpeted the forest floor in red and gold. She was close now, further through the woods she travelled until suddenly there it was...

"I'VE FOUND IT, IT'S THERE.......IT'S THERE!", she shrieked. She'd seen the village beyond the woods and the fair-haired boy with his horrible, unworthy hands caressing the sphere. Her sphere.. His dirty hands would soon be prised from it, the snatcher would be able to crack his fist like a nut.

The snatchers jumped around her, hissing their delight. Soon she would be free. Her evil heart beat fast, night would soon be falling and her snatchers would once again be able to begin their hunt except this time the prize was so much more valuable. The wait was unbearable, she knew that the coming days would seem the longest of the many she had already endured.

14.

All the children of the village held hands and formed a circle around the tree. There were about thirty of them dressed in the traditional costumes, Julie's little eyes peered through her loosely fitting lamb costume and shone with real happiness. The youngest of the children was little John Woods who was only four and he looked up at his proud parents, a little afraid and confused. Wendy was fourteen now and she savoured the opportunity of holding Peter's hand. He was only a little younger than her and she had made very sure of her place in the circle next to him. She tried not to make it too obvious how happy she was or the other children would probably tease her but she squeezed his hand tight and her heart beat with a nervous excitement. The children started to spin around the tree and the villagers watched and cheered, even Mr. Forthright looked as though he was enjoying it. Jacob began the song as usual and as soon as he launched into the first note the whole village joined him.

> 'Spin, Spin around the tree,
> You give us all we ever need.
> Your wood provides us sanctuary
> Your earth is kind and good to me'

And so they all sang, cheered and danced. The children spun faster and faster until poor old little John couldn't keep up. Eventually they all ended up in a heap on the floor, laughing and smiling. Luke stood holding his wife's hand and watching his three children. He turned to his wife and kissed her.

James found himself unable to get into the spirit of things. It wasn't that he didn't enjoy it, he just had the strangest feeling that he was being watched. He felt very anxious and scared as if he was being hunted by the night itself. He ran over to his dad who put his arm round him and he immediately felt a little safer. There was so much he wanted to tell his dad, he wanted to tell him that he was scared but instead he just looked up and smiled. James was changing, he could feel it but didn't know how exactly. For the last couple of nights he had felt that the sphere was trying to talk to him, to warn him. He longed to see that strange old man and his dog again. He didn't know why but he really missed them and he had so many things to ask him. Questions that he somehow felt only the old man could answer. He needed someone to talk to, the weight of his secret hung heavy from his shoulders, he reached into his pocket again and that familiar surge of energy coursed through his body.

It had taken Bugatti weeks of meditation and deep contemplation before he could be sure. Too many old emotions had re-surfaced and cluttered his normally clear mind. Now though there was no doubting it, his greatest fear had been realised. Zelda was still alive. Somehow after all these years she had resurfaced, been re-born. It had been a long, long time since he had felt her presence and he had hoped never to feel it again. He had watched as Zelda and her companions had destroyed the very world and magical institution he had loved. How her thirst for power had murdered the woman he loved, betrayed him and all those of his order. He had watched her die, he had watched through teary eyes as she had burned all those years ago. "It seems she was even more powerful than I feared", he thought to himself. He knew that even in his prime he would be no match for her but now he was just an old man, so out of practice that he scarcely thought of himself as a magician anymore. He would be like a lamb to the slaughter, she would play with him like a cat tormenting a mouse. He knew that there was only one thing he could do, he would have to reach the Sacred Table. The Sacred Table was at least a month's relentless travel from here via horseback. Bugatti was in the flatlands to the east. He had come here to still his mind and to journey deep into the fifth element. There was something incredibly calming about the way the green landscape seemed to stretch on to infinity, perfectly flat in every direction, broken only by the odd cluster of trees. He turned his head up to the sky and let out a strange call. The noise spread out across the flat land far and wide, then he sat back down for he knew he could be waiting for a while for his call to be answered.

The whole village had now moved into the hall. The children were still wearing their costumes and the grown ups had dressed up for the masked ball. The masks were made of the most amazing colours. Bright, bright reds and deep, rich blues, emerald greens and turquoise. Four musicians were playing the old traditional barn dance songs as the colours of the masks and feet bounced around the room in perfect unison. James had his arms out in front of him and Lucy held tightly onto his outstretched hands. For a brief moment, as they spun around the room laughing to the music together, he thought of nothing else; he had almost completely forgotten about the mysterious little sphere that had been weighing on his mind so heavily for the past few months. Lucy's auburn hair was swinging wildly around her pretty little face and James felt happy. He barely even noticed his two sisters who were sat together in the corner looking at him and sniggering. If he had then he would have seen as Peter came up and took Wendy by the hand and he would have seen the look of delight on her face as he guided her shyly onto the dance floor. They too began to spin around together, cautiously at first but then, as they both became a little more confident, they began to turn faster and faster, losing themselves in the music and the fun and the laughter of the evening. As James was spinning with Lucy he suddenly caught the eye of Wendy across the room. For the tiny moment as they were both turning they shared a look and both of them knew exactly what it meant; maybe tonight would be the night for both of them after all!

As usual it was Dowser who first noticed the beautiful black stallion approaching. The huge, powerful horse was galloping towards them at an incredible pace. Even from a distance Bugatti could watch its muscles rippling with each great stride. He stood up to admire the creature effortlessly eating up the ground in front of him. The stallion came to an abrupt halt besides them and raised itself on to its back legs snorting. He looked absolutely magnificent, his glossy black coat shining with a thin layer of perspiration.

'Hello my friend", Bugatti said as he approached the beast. 'You're a fine looking fellow now aren't you?', he continued as he reached out, affectionately slapping him at the base of his thick neck. 'Thank you for coming so quickly, I'm afraid we have a long journey ahe...'

The old man shook. 'Oh dear!' A look of genuine concern swept across his face; James was in danger, he had sensed it instantly. He jumped up onto the horse's back in one smooth, graceful movement and then looked down at Dowser who suddenly looked so small and vulnerable below.

'Come my friends, there is no time to waste.' He dug his heels into the steed's side, 'I guess the Sacred Table will have to have to wait', he thought to himself as the ground passed beneath his feet.

15.

Already the celebrations of the night before seemed a distant memory. The dancing had gone on well into the night, their feet had shaken the very foundations of the village hall and their laughter filled the evening air. However tonight the same anxious fear had returned and seemed only to have grown now that there were no such distractions. It was a grey night with a strong, biting wind that hinted at the long winter still yet to come. Luke could tell that the children were scared, they seemed to talk of nothing other than these snatchers and he did his best to comfort them.

'Right, kids, it's time for bed now.'

The fire was burning its way through the last of the evening's logs.

'I don't want to go to bed, dad', Julie protested, 'what if the snatchers come for me?'

'No snatcher is going to be getting their hands on any of you three, not on my life' said Luke and gave them a great big smile.

James couldn't help but feel anxious. He did his best to hide it but something was troubling him, he just still couldn't shrug off the feeling that he was being watched, hunted, that something horrible was lurking just round every corner and that whatever it was was getting closer?...

'You OK, son?', Luke asked, walking over to rub James's hair 'You seem all out of sorts at the moment. Is it all these stories you've been hearing or are you just thinking about your kiss with Lucy?!' He went bright red in an instance. 'News travels fast in this village, my boy, and don't you forget it' Luke laughed. He looked up and smiled sheepishly at his dad. 'I'm fine', he said trying to change the conversation. 'Don't you worry about those snatchers, girls', desperately hoping to conceal his own fear, if they try to get us, then I'll fight them off.'.

'Ha ha, that's the spirit, my boy', laughed Luke. He playfully his son on the bum and went on, 'now - off to your room, sweethearts, and remember, the only thing to fear is fear itself. You'll be as safe as a duck in a storm in here, James'll see to that won't you my boy?!'

The children were all tucked up in bed when Luke brought the oil lamp in. He walked over to Julie's bed and set it on her bedside table. Poor little Julie was too scared to sleep in the dark so he'd filled the lamp with enough oil to burn through until the morning. One by one he kissed them all goodnight and gave them each a great big hug. James felt so safe wrapped up in that strong embrace and pushed his face into his dad's bushy beard.

'Night night, kids', called their mother who was busy tidying up outside.

Luke backed out of the room and quietly set their door on the latch.

The children lay in their separate beds unusually silent, each of them listening to every sound outside; desperately trying not to let their imaginations turn it into something dark and terrifying. With every rattle of the window their young hearts would beat a little faster but after a lot of tossing and turning eventually they began to fall asleep.

The snatchers moved hastily through the forest with their long capes brushing on its floor. The nights were growing long and had travelled for six of them, never tiring, their long scrawny limbs carrying them twice as fast as any man could travel. They stopped to burrow small, damp caves in the ground to protect them from the sunlight during the day. The snatchers, like all of Zelda's creations, were creatures of the night. The night brought with it a shadowy, half-lit world of imagination that would allow them to manifest. In the bright light of day these phantoms would simply disappear into a vapour of smoke. Zelda's magic wasn't strong enough to bring her creations into the daylight yet so for now they would have to lurk in the shadows where they belonged. They were reaching the edge of the forest and they could clearly make out where the trees ended and the fields began. Zelda had guided them perfectly from the floor of her perpetual cage. They stopped at the forest edge and gazed out on the sleeping village beyond, surveying the area, their claws flexing in anticipation. There it was, the little wooden house on the edge of the field. They hissed in excitement at the terror they were about to inflict and the joy they would bring their mistress when they returned with the sphere. The snatchers were hungry, the field in front was full of dozing sheep and they eyed them up greedily. The wind was blowing a strong south-easterly wind which kept the snatchers foul stench from filling the village, Zelda had seen to that.

They crept silently along the edge of the field, careful not to alarm the sheep. Their pale, hooked noses protruded from the hoods of their capes and their tongues flicked at the air. They were so close now, they could almost taste the children in the air. They silently glided under a wooden fence and into a paddock. Suddenly the snatchers stopped, a little white horse had appeared from within a small wooden shelter in the field.

Meg had awoken instantly, she didn't know if it had been her old ears or sensitive nose but something had caused sufficient alarm for her to leave the comfort of her straw bed. The night was blowing a cold wind and she sleepily stumbled out into the paddock, her ears twisting and turning. Suddenly she caught sight of the sinister shadows out of the corner of her big round eyes and immediately tried to raise the alarm. She grunted and groaned and shrieked as loud as she could but she was just too far from the house to wake them inside. The snatchers moved through the paddock as quickly as possible where the little white horse was rearing and pacing and snorting. They were close now, the paddock lay behind them and as far as they could tell the village still slept peacefully. They were approaching the house from the large garden beside. Luke briefly stirred in his sleep and for the short moment he was conscious he caught a faint hint of a foul smell. The cat must have brought a dead animal into the house, he thought to himself sleepily and rather than go and have a look he decided to leave it until the morning, rolled over and was soon snoring lightly again. The snatchers came to a wooden outhouse and peered through the glass window. The window had been covered with a dark fabric. Their great big eyes were so accustomed to the dark that, through the tiniest hole in the cloth, they could just about make out what lay inside. They saw that it was the home of a metal worker. They could smell the oil and see the pots and pans and spears and daggers gleaming gently amongst the shadows. Zelda could have her uses for a man with such skills they thought to themselves. He would make a valuable servant or an unwanted enemy. They all hissed quietly in agreement.

They had reached the house and lifted their noses to take in deep breaths of the air. Their long, forked tongues darting in and out from between their sharp teeth to try and get a better taste of the scent. They split up. Two of them carried on quietly making their way around the side of the house, looking in each window they passed. The other two crept straight up to the front door and slowly eased it open. The house, like all the others in the village was more of a log cabin or a bungalow than a house as we know one. Beautifully crafted out of the forest wood and ever so slightly raised up off the ground by small stilts. They were inside now and quickly moved through the kitchen and sitting room. The floorboards creaked quietly underfoot but not enough to wake anyone. They found themselves in a small corridor with a door immediately to the left of them and another at the other end to the right. The snatcher who was leading knelt down and put it's nose to the crack under the door. It could hear the light snoring and smell the manly scent escaping through the crack. They rose and carried on moving silently down the corridor until they reached the partially opened door. A faint light was coming from the room. Slowly and carefully its fingers wrapped around the the door and the talons left small, deep indentations in the wood

Meanwhile the other two had made their way to the children's window. The room was lit by one small flame and they could easily make out the three children sleeping. The one closest to the window was very young. Her blood would be full of life and would feed Zelda well. It wouldn't take more than one of them to take the carrier they thought to themselves.

Wendy's sleep had been restless and she began to stir awake. Instantly the foul stench of death and decay hit her and her heart almost stopped dead with fear. Her senses told her immediately that something was very wrong. She looked up in the gently lit room and what she saw was so frightening that she didn't even know if she could scream. The long bony fingers with their sharp clawed talons, each one looked as sharp and deadly as an eagle's beak had wrapped around the door and it was starting to open. It took a little while for the scream to come but when it did, it was the most piercing and loudest scream any girl had ever made. Her body shook with the exertion and fear. The whole house woke instantly and Luke was up and out of his bed, heading to his door before he'd even had time to open his eyes, the stench almost choking him. James looked up and couldn't believe his eyes. It was like waking into the most horrifying nightmare. He watched as Julie was ripped from her bed and pulled out of the window. Their hands had totally smothered her and she couldn't even make a sound but he could see the terror in her eyes as theirs briefly met and it chilled him to bone. As she was pulled out her foot caught the oil lamp and it fell to the floor. The burning oil smashed and spat across the ground and the flames began to leap up from the floor. It was all happening so quickly that it was impossible to take it all in, shock had overcome him. James sat up like a coiled spring and turned to the door. There he saw two of the most vicious, evil looking creatures, far worse than his imagination ever could have prepared him for come running straight at him. Their cold, piercing eyes bore into him from long white faces with features that resembled something like that of wax dripping from a candle; forked tongues flicked between their sharp, cracked teeth. Before he could move the first hand had grabbed him by the throat and lifted him up out of the bed. He was choking. He could feel the other one's hand scratching deep into his pocket, its sharp claw breaking his skin. Bugatti's words were rushing through his mind. He kicked and fought but they were just too strong. His heart was beating so loudly that it felt as if his head was going to burst. He couldn't bear the thought of those filthy fingers clutching at his perfect sphere. He kicked out hard again and caught the snatcher in the chest but the life was being squeezed out of him and his kicks had little effect. All the time the flames were growing around him and the room was filling with smoke. He felt the very moment the sphere was ripped from his pocket, he sensed a sadness that seemed to come from the sphere itself. He wanted to scream but the long fingers were wrapped so tightly around his throat that he couldn't even breathe, let alone make a sound. He didn't want to show the creature that he was afraid, he didn't want to give it the satisfaction but his eyes betrayed him. The snatchers cold, dead eyes stared straight through him as it squeezed harder, eagerly waiting for the moment he would go limp in its hands and it relished in the fear it could see etched all over his young face.

Suddenly Luke came bursting in through the door. He didn't have time to be scared of the creatures. He saw Julie's empty bed and James being held up in the air by his throat, choked and nearly lifeless. He threw himself at the snatcher holding his son and knocked it to the ground. James fell back down to the bed gasping for air. The thick smoke burnt its way into his lungs in fast, hard breaths.

'RUN!' Luke screamed. 'RUN...Now.' A snatcher leapt on him from behind and James watched his dad's big strong legs buckle under its weight. Luke screamed as it sunk its razor sharp teeth deep into his shoulder. He dipped forwards and managed to throw the beast onto the burning floor but it had taken a large chunk of his flesh with it. Almost immediately another was on him, its claws slashed across his chest and the snatchers seemed invigorated by the sight of the fresh blood that was now flowing freely. The flames had begun to lick their way up the walls, and James crawled towards the doorway, coughing. His eyes were streaming tears, a combination of the fear and the smoke. The air was so thick that it was hard to make out any more than the silhouette of his father fighting so bravely. Wendy was screaming hysterically as she watched the snatchers' savage attack. They were on him again, clawing, biting but each time he would knock them back into the flames with his big strong fists, tears were streaming down her helpless face. Luke managed to hold the snatchers just long enough for Theresa to come running in hysterical with shock and fear through the smoke to grab their screaming daughter by the hand. She dragged her out of the room and pulled her into the corridor. She couldn't bear watching her husband being torn apart in front of her eyes and she ran back into the room. One of the snatchers had its hand wrapped around Luke's neck, an animal instinct overcame her and she bit down hard into the gristly skin. It tasted like rotten meat but the snatcher loosened its tight grip just long enough for Luke to free himself and land a heavy kick into its gut. With one strong arm he forced his wife back out of the room but another of the snatchers charged at him and sent him crashing into the wall behind. He turned to look at his screaming wife, his eyes stinging with the smoke, 'GO!.......LEAVE ME!' he screamed. All the bedclothes had caught fire and the room was unbearably hot but he waded back in, fists blindly throwing punches at the monsters whose claws were ripping and tearing at his skin.

Another snatcher was squeezing its way in through the window, its cold eyes longing for blood. All three of them were on him now. He tried to keep fighting but he was getting weaker with every blow, scratch and bite he took. One of them was trying to make its way past him to get at James. From somewhere, sheer desperation and the need to protect his beloved son he found some extra strength and beat the snatcher back down. He turned and looked straight at his son with his brave eyes which were normally so full of joy and love. He couldn't even manage to shout, 'go……..please…..just go'.

James took one more look at his valiant father fighting so bravely but had to turn away as he saw those foul fingers wrapping their way around his throat. He heard the thud as they brought him to his knees but he couldn't bring himself to look anymore. He had fought so courageously but there were just too many of them and he was slowly being overcome. James turned to his mum and sister whose shocked faces were wet with tears. He took them both by the hand and together they ran.

16.

Bugatti had been riding as hard as his poor horse could take for the past six days and nights. Sleeping only briefly in between and stopping only when it was absolutely essential that they eat, drink and rest. Dowser had run by his side, giving every last ounce of his energy to try and keep up. Fields and villages and woods and hills had passed them by in a blur. Night had fallen long ago but still they rode on. The horse's tired hooves continued to beat hard on the ground but he knew that there was still much ground left to cover.

He looked back at his tired old friend struggling so hard to keep up. Their eyes met and Bugatti knew that Dowser would follow him to his own death if he just asked. The wind blew fiercely through his long grey hair and his overcoat whipped and slapped behind him. He feared that he was already too late nevertheless there was not a second that could be wasted.

13.

The house stood burning. The fire had spread from the bedroom and was fast engulfing the whole building. The flames danced high into the dark night sky and the heat was unbearable. The house would soon be little more than a pile of dark charred ashes and the flames would devour not only the house but also the body of Luke Shears, the brave father and husband, along with it. The scene was like no other the villagers had witnessed and many of them stood silently, the others sobbing quietly, staring at the flames as if they couldn't believe the sight before them. The roar of the fire and the cries of scared children filled the air. Jacob had his big arms wrapped around Theresa in a desperate attempt to console her and a few villagers were delicately placing warm rugs around the distraught children's shoulders. As they watched the flames hungrily consume the house they all quietly thought of the two that were missing; that greatly loved, brave, kind man and his tiny, helpless daughter.

'They've taken her.....they've taken her'. Jacob held Theresa tight and felt every inch of her sorrow shaking between his arms, for it may have been the Shears' house that was burning but the whole village shared in their grief and their loss and their fear. James had no more tears left to cry, it was too much for him and his sister Wendy to even comprehend, the shock had been so great that their young minds had been numbed by the utter horror of it all, they simply stood with the heat burning their skin, watching as it destroyed all that they had ever known. The smoke carried with it the innocence of their childhood and they would never be the same again.

Bugatti had seen the flames light up the sky from a long distance away and he knew then that he was already too late. The eerie orange glow that hovered on the horizon drove him on and his desperately tired horse managed to find some extra reserves of energy from somewhere. It galloped faster and faster and poor Dowser was falling gradually further behind. The long journey had taken its toll on him and each step of his furry legs was a struggle but he fought with every strained muscle in his body to keep up with his master as best he could. That hour chasing the horizon was the longest of any Bugatti could remember but finally he broke through the forest and saw the village spread out before him. As he rode towards the burning house he slowed down so as not to alarm the already frightened villagers. They were still standing around the house, many of them were returning with buckets of water from the pond, desperately trying to stem the fury of the fire but it was of no use. The heat was too great and the flames too strong. The water only served to create a thick black smoke that hung in the air around them. The villagers were so captivated by the site and the horror of the evening that at first they barely noticed the old man approaching them on his strong, resplendent horse. It was James who saw him first. He could make out the shadowy silhouette of the old man dismounting from his horse and knew immediately that it was Bugatti. He had never been so grateful to see anyone before and threw the rug from his shoulders and as he turned to run into his arms the dam burst and the tears came flooding down his face. Even though they'd only met once James felt a love for Bugatti and his dog as if he'd known them for years. The man held him and James felt like a tiny child in the sanctuary of his arms. He looked up at the man's kindly face and wept. 'They killed men dad, they taken Julie and the sphere' he sobbed, 'they've taken everything'. Bugatti didn't say anything but there was something in his eyes that felt soothing and calming to the frightened boy. It was the first time since the horrible events began that he'd thought about his precious sphere because as dear as it may have been to him it meant nothing compared to all else he had lost. The memory of the sphere had been cast aside by the heartbreaking memory of watching his fearless father being torn apart by those creatures. He didn't long for the sphere as he longed for his father and his little sister but the thought of it being in the hands of the snatchers made him feel physically sick. He imagined poor little Julie being carried away and his tears and sorrow were replaced by an anger and hatred that welled up from deep inside him. 'You must not let them turn your heart', the old man whispered in his ear as if he had been reading the young boys mind, 'hatred leads you down a path with only one end, a path that leads only to bitterness and sorrow, instead feel the love you have for your sister and send it to her'. Bugatti rubbed the top of James's head and knelt down to look him straight in the eye. 'Now dry your eyes, i'm afraid we have little time for tears, not whilst there's still a chance to save your sister. It must not be in her hands for long', he added almost to himself. 'We must leave immediately'. On that he stood up to his full height and turned his gaze to face the rest of the villagers who now looked on.

He took James by the hand and together they walked towards his weeping mother and sister who stood in the middle of the gathering. Theresa had a protective arm over Wendy's shoulder and they both gazed at the approaching man through sad, wet eyes. Bugatti had seen that exact same look many years ago and he wished that somehow he could change it but he knew of no magic great enough to cure a broken heart. Even from that distance Theresa could make out a kindness in the eyes of the approaching man. The villagers let him pass through and watched on, unsure what to make of the stranger. It was Bugatti who spoke first. He spoke directly to the mother who had lost so much.

'I too have lost those closest to me and my heart shares the heavy burden of loss that I know you must feel. There is little comfort that may be found in words at such a time but if my words can bring you anything then I long that they may bring you hope. For it is my resolve to return your daughter safely back to you'. His words were calm and measured yet forceful. 'There is still time to save your daughter and that is precisely what I intend to do'. She looked into his eyes and for some reason she trusted him. Maybe it was just her desperate longing to see her beautiful little girl again but when the man spoke she believed him, more importantly for some inexplicable reason she believed that he could do it. 'I cannot do this without the help of your son. I'm sure you have many, many questions but I'm afraid your questions will have to wait, for every minute is one we cannot afford to lose. Every minute your daughter is being taken further away from here, further into the unknown. There are powers at work here that I cannot begin to explain to you but I need you to trust me. It is James's fate to ride with me'.

Jacob stepped in to speak at once. 'If you are going then we'll go with you'.

Bugatti turned his steady gaze to meet that of the tall man who had just spoken. 'Brave man, I have no doubt that you would give your own life to save the girl but for now there is nothing more you can do. Comfort the mother and child.'

'Who was this strange man who spoke to him with such authority?', Jacob thought to himself, but this was no time for pride. 'You're an old man like me, you will need people to fight for you', he blasted back in retort.

At this Bugatti smiled. He looked up to the skies and with his outstretched finger he made a strange gesture to the stars which hung above the burning house. The villagers watched in fascination beginning to wonder if the old man was totally mad as his finger drew small, imaginary circles in the night shy. As if from nowhere a black rain cloud had begun to form. It took a while for them all to notice but there was no mistaking when it burst. The rain came falling to the ground around them thick and hard. Almost instantly the flames of the burning house were subdued. A thick choking cloud of smoke was coming towards them. Bugatti held out an outstretched palm and it was as if a wind came from within him. The smoke came no further and began to blow back into the fields behind.

They all stood there silent, not believing what they had just seen. Bugatti looked straight at Jacob with his fierce, powerful eyes. His hair was wet with the heavy rain that fell. 'There is nothing more that you can do to help me', he said softly. 'If there was then I would certainly ask for your assistance. All that you must do is what comes naturally to you I'm sure. Look after the mother and the child and try to comfort them for such wounds will not easily heal.'. He turned once more to look at Theresa and her sad daughter who clung on to her slight frame as tightly as she could. 'Theresa' he almost whispered now. 'I need your consent for James to ride with me, we must find your daughter, if I could go alone I would'. 'Just look after him' she wept 'I can't lose another, and bring them back, bring them back safe to me'. He didn't say anything more for there was nothing more to say, his eyes had said it all for him and theirs had already told him everything. Meanwhile Dowser had finally made his way to his master's side and Bugatti reached down to pat his panting head with that strong, loving hand of his. Then together they turned, the old man, the boy and the dog and headed back out towards the awaiting horse.

James turned to face his mother one last time and then turned to the old man. 'Come, it's time to leave', Bugatti said and together they headed towards the field beyond the house.

17.

It had been a long time since Meg had been asked to do anything except eat hay and graze in the field but she seemed more than willing to offer James her old back. Bugatti spoke to him as he fixed the saddle to her. 'The sphere is a part of you now. You are its true carrier and it will be calling for you., allow the fifth element to guide you to the sphere'. 'But I don't know how. I don't know where they've taken it'. Bugatti's eyes suddenly turned sharp and fierce. In an instant James felt small and young again in his presence. 'There is no time for this James. You know how and you will lead us there'

They both mounted their horses and Dowser readied his weary legs once again for another long run. Meg looked so tiny and old standing next to Bugatti's great stead but James was glad to have her with him. He was soon to be leaving all else that he knew behind him so he was grateful for Meg's familiar presence on this journey into the unknown. He was anxious and afraid. How could he know which way they had gone or how to find them? He looked down at the ground for any signs or marking that may help to indicate the way but he could see nothing. The night was dark and the light of the burning house was too far behind them.

'It is not your reason that will guide you, it is your feelings, it is your love.' Bugatti's words made no sense to him, how could his feelings lead him to Julie? He felt so alone and lost up there on Meg's back and they hadn't even left the village yet. He looked back at the charred remains of his old house and he thought of all he'd lost. 'James!', Bugatti barked and instantly he snapped back to the moment. 'Let these feelings go. Let them pass through or they will cloud your mind and corrupt your judgement. Your love will guide you. The sphere is calling you. Shhhhh...' He held his finger up to his bearded mouth. 'Can you hear it whispering to you in the wind?' James was silent but he could hear nothing. 'Your sister needs you. Simply trust your intuition and you'll not go far wrong', Bugatti said with a smile. James knew that he was right, his sister did need him and he would find her, somehow. He didn't know how but he was going to bring back, he was going to rescue her somehow. The thought of her being carried away took him from his own worries and fears and filled him with a new sense of purpose. He didn't know which way they had gone but they had to have gone somewhere and every second he waited was one he could have spent searching. He tugged gently on Meg's reigns and turned towards an opening in the forest. He looked only onwards, never turning back and together they left the village fields behind them.

For the most part they rode through the night in silence. Each of them lost in their own thoughts. Bugatti was uneasy. He didn't know how she'd returned but there was no denying her presence. He had left her behind a long time ago yet somehow it seemed her spirit had managed to live on. Zelda had the power to create life and he knew that if she were allowed to have her way the world would bear little resemblance to the beautiful one that they were riding through tonight. He knew that she would be able to sense him easily and that he must disguise himself if they were to remain hidden from her gaze. Even after all this time his presence would be too familiar to her, too easy to find. He knew that he must lose himself, he must hold his attention elsewhere. Cut off his thoughts and lead the essence of his being to a place far away from here, somewhere she couldn't find. The forest track was narrow and James led out in front with Bugatti and Dowser following closely behind.

'James, you must lead us, I can be of no help to you now. I must leave you or I will be putting the whole mission at risk'. James turned sharply to look back at the old man. 'No! You can't leave me.' His voice wavered somewhat with the sudden fear he felt at being left alone in this dark woodland with those creatures somewhere out there. 'I need you.'

'I don't have time to explain fully; I will still be here, my body will ride behind you, you will not be alone, but my attention and my spirit must be elsewhere. Besides you will still have Dowser.' With that the shaggy haired dog came trotting up beside him as if on cue. He was panting but he looked up at James with the smiling, innocent eyes that only a dog can possess. 'I will return in a while but for now our fate is in your hands.' If James had still been looking behind him he would have seen the moment Bugatti's attention left. The man's body almost flickered in the moonlight now, it possessed a strange sort of transparency, a constitution much like that which we imagine of a ghost.

They had been riding for several hours now and were deep in the heart of the forest. The track was narrow and branches stretched out overhead. Every so often they would come to a fork in the path and each of these moments presented James with a crucial decision. It should have been a difficult decision, whether to go left or right and although he was always anxious as he approached them the closer he got the more appealing one of the paths would seem. He couldn't explain it. Perhaps it was the way the moonlight had broken through the canopy above or maybe it was the shapes in the shadows that drew him one way another but for some reason each time a particular route just seemed to feel better. It was only afterwards that he would find himself doubting his decision, wondering whether or not he was going the right way. Bugatti was of no help at all. It was so dark and the path so narrow that James had to keep his attention on what lay immediately in front of him. There was no easy opportunity for him to look back but the sound of the mighty horse's steps behind him let him know that the old man was never far behind.

He could see another fork in the track approaching but this time he really had no idea which way to go. As he got closer his doubt grew even more and he began to convince himself that he had got them both completely lost. He began to cry quietly for his little sister, certain that he had let her down and that there was no way he could ever find her. Both paths lead simply to yet more darkness and he thought that each step must have been taking them further from his sister, further from where they needed to be. Maybe it was his tears that had awakened the strange sleeping spectre of the old man behind him for suddenly he spoke. 'Well done James. We must find somewhere to get some rest for a few hours, you are tired.'

'We're completely lost', replied James, his voice shaking as he tried to hide his tears.

'And what makes you so sure of that?', came the rich, deep voice from the shadows. 'Do you know which way they went?'

'No, I don't have a clue, that's the whole point. That's why this is so stupid. We should have taken everyone from the village with us and then we could all be looking for her.' The young boy couldn't hide his frustration any longer and tears rolled freely down his cheeks.

'Well, if you don't know which way they went then how could you possibly know that they didn't come this way? I see no reason to assume that we are not exactly where we need to be. Now let's get some rest'.

James didn't know what to say to that. He supposed that perhaps there was the smallest chance that they might have gone this way. It wasn't much to go on but at least it gave him a little hope. Just enough for his tired eyes to dry.

'Now, quickly, we must find some soft ground on which to rest. I will need to form a protective circle immediately to hide us from her gaze. Let your eyes guide you'.

'Guide me to what?', replied James.

'To the perfect resting place of course', came the answer. 'Scan the forest quickly and follow your feelings'.

James was too tired to argue, anywhere would do. He could probably sleep right here on Meg's back if he needed to but he quickly did what the old man had asked. As he turned he could just about make out a small clearing in the trees to his left. It looked as though there might be the outline of a fallen tree. He gave Meg's reins a gentle tug and they headed slowly through the woodland.

James was right, there had been a little clearing and the ground was covered in a soft moss, which was surprisingly comfortable to sit on. He had busied himself collecting old, dead bits of wood for a fire as Bugatti had instructed whilst the old man had been carefully scraping a perfect circle into the ground around them with a stick he had found in the area where they now sat.

'You have managed to find us a fine spot James, I have absolute faith that your intuition has lead you correctly.' James didn't share the man's confidence. The night was cold, he hadn't really noticed until now but he began to shiver and once again it was if the man was reading his mind.

'Right, let's get this fire started then', he said. 'Do you know how to set a good fire?', he asked.

'I can make a good fire, my Dad showed me how.' Even just the mention of his father was like a knife to his heart. He felt a deep burning hatred for those creatures that had savaged his father, his hero, and his mind was riddled with guilt for not being able to do more to help him, for not being stronger for letting his fear get the better of him. His chest felt hollow as if there was a huge, gaping hole where his heart used to be. He set about placing the logs in the way his father had shown him, trying to take his mind as far away from the feelings he was immersed in but there was no escaping them. He positioned the logs in a triangle so that the air could circulate underneath the flames. When he was done Bugatti stood up as if to inspect his work.

'Very good', he said. 'Now I bet your father never showed you this.' And with that he slowly passed his hand over the top of the dead, dry wood, which immediately burst into flames. The sudden heat flushed against the boy's face and he had to lean back to distance himself from it.

'Now you're just showing off', he said with a cheeky little smile on his face.

'I suppose I am', replied the old man. He caught the boy's eye as he said it and they laughed together, laughed as much as his sorrow would allow.

Bugatti looked over at him and his eyes shone with a greater intensity than the glowing embers which sparked forth from the flames of the fire between them.

'When we first met you told me that you had never seen the sea.'

James was a little puzzled by the sudden change of conversation but was happy for the brief respite it brought him from his own thoughts.

'That's right, I've never seen the sea', he replied absent-minded, still slightly distracted by all that was going on inside his troubled head.

'You have spent your life at sea, James'. He looked out at the man whose face seemed so familiar and tried to see if his eyes could offer any greater meaning to such a strange statement but they were serious and stern. 'We all spend our lives at sea', he went on. 'We are born at sea. It is only through death that we ever truly reach the land'.

There was a long pause, a pause which told him he was meant to ponder on the statement, a pause he was becoming more accustomed to the longer he spent with this strange man. James was so tired though that the words simply passed over him and dissipated into the night behind. Bugatti leaned forwards close to the fire and his face lit up with the warm light making the lines look deeper and more pronounced. He couldn't help but notice that the old man's eyes looked more mysterious than ever and he wondered if he would ever truly understand the great many riddles that fell so gracefully from his lips. 'You have been at sea your whole life', he repeated once more. 'You are battling the seas right this very moment, let me show you'.

18

Julie had never felt so scared or alone in her whole short life. She couldn't even bring herself to look at the creature that held her against its cold skin. It held her tightly under the stinking, coarse cape that flapped in the wind and whipped against her soft, young cheeks. The snatcher wore a small pouch made of animal skin that hung around its neck. There was clearly something solid inside as Julie could hear a soft thud as it beat against its chest with every step but the fear she felt kept her from giving it much attention. It seemed as though she was in a terrible dream yet it was a nightmare that exceeded the limits of her young imagination. All those nights that she had lain in bed imagining what the snatchers were like could never have prepared her for the terrifying reality that she found herself confronted with. She had cried great big muffled cries ever since that moment she had been torn from her bed. The tears seemed endless and thoughts of the smoke and the house she'd watched burn filled her mind as the snatcher carried her ever further into the distance. She pleaded with the snatcher but it was silent, immune to her hurt and to her tears. The only reply was the steady hiss of its breath, and the rhythmic soft thud as it ran tirelessly through the black night. Through her sodden, exhausted eyes she could see that the sun was starting to rise. The snatcher seemed to pick up speed, running as if it was racing against the rising sun. The woods rushed past her and occasionally a thorn or a twig would scratch her skin and she would scream out with fresh pain.

She tried not to imagine where she was being taken but every long stride was a step further from the home and family she loved, each one robbed her of what little hope remained and replaced it with despair. Suddenly the snatcher began to slow. It was sniffing the air, searching for a scent. She closed her eyes tightly and cried, wondering if she'd ever see her family again. It was all too much as the snatcher ducked down and forced her roughly into a tight dark hole in the forest floor. The smell was unbearable. It pushed her in further until she felt her body pressing against another. She could feel cold fur against her skin and the smell of festering meat. The floor was sticky with the blood of whichever poor creature lay next to her. The snatcher quickly covered the top of the hole with branches, leaves and dirt until it was completely black and she was alone in the darkness with nothing but the sound of breath hissing through her captor's long nose and that of her tiny beating heart. 'This is it', she thought to herself, 'I'm going to be eaten just like this thing next to me'. She must have passed out from the fear and the exhaustion for when she woke she could make out an eerie glow escaping from the top of the pouch that hung from the sleeping snatchers sinewy neck. It lit up the creature's features just enough for her heart to stop dead. The full horror of the evening's events came rushing back to her. The subsequent futile scream which wailed from her mournful mouth was soon swallowed by an empty forest and an uncaring, clawed hand.

Julie had lost count of the nights she had spent cramped in different holes and caves across the land. She had almost begun to forget what sunlight felt like against her skin. She was so weak and hungry that much of the journey had passed in a blur but her fear and sorrow only grew with each passing day. She longed to be wrapped up in the warm, strong, comforting arms of her father or to be sitting next to the roaring log fire with her brother and sister but that seemed like a lifetime ago. The snatcher had stopped occasionally by a river or a spring and dunked her head into the water and she would swallow as much as she could without choking. At night the snatcher would rip flesh from a freshly slain animal and force the bloody raw meat down her throat and she hated it all the more for it. She no longer cried for she knew that her tears served only to satisfy the monster that held her. Instead she sat silently, searching her mind for any remnants of hope that still remained.

The snatcher had carried her deep into a forest but it was unlike any forest she'd ever seen. The vast dead trees that towered above were so huge and imposing that she hid her eyes behind the snatchers coarse cape. She kept expecting to wake up and kept telling herself that it was just a horrible dream. But the stench and the touch of cold skin seemed very real even if the dead forest did not. After hours of running they finally stopped. She pushed aside the cape and tried to look at her surroundings but it was so dark that it took a while for her eyes to adjust. She could just about make out the silhouette of a gigantic tree but it was so tall that she couldn't even see where it ended. She was shivering, but it wasn't the cold this time. She was shivering at the sight of the tree; it was as if the tree itself was alive, alive with a very real evil; an evil that filled the air around her and flooded her lungs. The snatcher carried her closer to the vast dead trunk. It was as wide as her house back in the village and loomed up above her higher than she could even imagine. She held onto the creature tightly as if by reflex for she didn't know what she was more afraid of, the snatcher or that dark dead tree. They squeezed through the smallest crack in the wood and she found herself at the top of a long tunnel. The faint glow of firelight shone in the depths below but it brought her no comfort for she knew that they were going no further than this. They had arrived and she was soon to share the fate of the many other children that had come before her.

The snatcher went running down the tunnel, hissing with excitement, eager to bring Zelda what she so desperately sought. It had been the first of the snatchers to return but the others couldn't be too far behind. Julie looked up and the light that shone from the pouch lit up the snatchers pale skin. The tunnel opened up into a large cavern. The smouldering embers of a fire sat in the middle and gave just enough light for Julie to make out that there were at least another three tunnels running from this main chamber. In the far left of the room a dead deer hung by its feet from the ceiling and next to it were two cages made from cleanly stripped bones. They had been crudely put together and were clearly not the work of great craftsmen but they were effective enough.

As her captor carried her past the fire to the awaiting cage there was a brief moment where the embers warmed her skin reminding her of home and the long winter nights she would spend with her family. The memories of home brought fresh tears to her eyes and she fought hard not to sob aloud. The snatcher hurriedly threw her into the cage and slid a bone into a clasp to lock her inside and quickly turned to move to the opposite side of the cave. It was so dark down there that even with the faint glow of fiery embers it was almost impossible for her to make anything out. But then she saw it and it gave her the greatest shock since the first evening she'd been taken. She could make out what looked like a woman, the silhouette of her naked breasts was framed against the muddy wall and long dark hair framed a pale face. Even from this distance it was clear to see she was beautiful but then the silhouette changed and where there should have been legs there was a tangle of tree roots and bark. She could just about see where the roots and skin met and merged and then the horror that enveloped her was so great that suddenly she felt all consciousness drain from her hungry and exhausted body and she fell into the sodden earth that waited hungrily beneath her.

'Where is it....where is it?', she didn't shriek or shout with excitement as you may have expected. Instead her voice was almost quiet but it trembled with agitation and longing. The snatcher reached into the pouch that hung from its neck. Zelda watched every move getting frustrated as the snatcher fumbled around. She held out her one shaking hand that wasn't chained to the earth. 'Give it to me', her voice was slightly more raised this time. 'GIVE IT TO ME!' She screamed it this time and the piercing shriek continued to bounce of the walls long after it had been uttered. And then there it was. The snatcher placed it in her hand and she could immediately feel the surge of power it contained flow through her.

All those centuries she had waited. Every torturing second that passed spent rooted to the dirt below and here it was in the palm of her hand. She no longer had an eye for beauty, she barely even appreciated the soft hues which danced so delicately inside the sphere. It was the power she longed for and that was all that the sphere was to her, a source of yet more power. It felt exactly as she had imagined and she could feel all the force and magic locked inside, the power that could finally free her from the muddy prison that had held her for all this time. She closed her eyes and took in a long satisfied breath. She was so close, the sphere was hers, now she must simply work out how to unlock the secret of its power.

19

Bugatti had left the fire and vanished into the shadows of the woodland beyond. The air was still, with only the occasional gust of wind rattling its way through the trees and playing with the open flames. However, James's mind was far from still. His heart was filled with a sorrow he had never felt before, his loss made even greater by the fact that he had witnessed his father's tragic fight and watched as his young sister was torn from her bed. The sorrow was so great that it had mixed with anger, an emotion he could somehow relate to more than the deep hurt that was still so raw and unknown. He wasn't scared of those creatures anymore, he longed for them. He longed to see them so that he could hurt them, destroy them and make them suffer. He was almost shaking with this strange cocktail of rage and sorrow when Bugatti returned from the woodland. He was carrying a great big, straight piece of wood. It must have been a very straight branch that had fallen somewhere in the forest. It was almost twice as tall as him and as wide as his neck but Bugatti didn't struggle, he seemed to carry it as if it were any other piece of firewood. He approached James silently without giving any explanation for the huge piece of wood and he watched on curiously. When he was only a few feet away from the boy he lifted the pole high up into the air vertically above his head and suddenly, with the most explosive movement he forced it downwards. There was an almighty thud and the whole ground shook beneath them as the wood struck and pierced its way deep into the hard earth. James couldn't believe that a man could do that. It was as if he had just stuck a knife into butter. The pole was now set straight in the ground. Bugatti gave it a shake and James looked on in amazement, it seemed as solid as the trees that surrounded them. Bugatti looked at the boy and smiled with mischievous eyes as he caught the bewildered expression on his young, stunned face.

'Stand up, James, and come wrap your hands around the mast of your ship.' James's first reaction was to feel angry with the old man for he knew only too well that he had just lost his father and more than likely his sister too. He knew that he had only recently watched his house burn to the ground and he must have known that he wasn't in the mood for silly, childish games.

'Stand up, James, and wrap your hands tightly around your mast.' This time though there was no look of humour in his eyes, the tone was firm and James stood slowly and more than a little begrudgingly. He held the pole that was now set firmly between them and felt the rigidity of it. Bugatti lent forwards and suddenly without warning pushed him forcefully in the chest and he lost his grip instantly falling to the ground.

'What did you do that for?', James shouted angrily at the old fool. 'What sort of stupid game is this?'

'I told you to hold it tight.' Bugatti's voice wasn't raised but somehow it felt as though it was. 'If that had been a wave then you would have been lost. The water would have ripped you from your ship and you would be struggling for breath, fighting a losing battle with the currents in a cold sea. We are not messing around here, I don't play games, the stakes are too high for that'.

James glared at him but stood up and once again took his place by the pole. This time however he held tight, waiting for the next part of this stupid game.

'Our spirits are divided amongst a great many different dimensions. These dimensions are separate and yet the same and to understand that is a lifetime's work on its own.' Bugatti's face was close now, so close that he barely only whispered the words but the proximity didn't help to bring them any clarity. 'We live our lives simultaneously in a great may different realities. You know only of this one because our consciousness remains firmly routed in the reality of the senses, what we can see, what we touch and what we taste. The sleeping mind presents us with a many different realities, you experience much of this through your dreams although I'm sure like most men you do not give them the attention that they warrant. In order to truly reach your full potential you must learn to master all realities within all dimensions.'

James was just simply lost now, he had no idea at all what the old man was saying and could scarcely be bothered to listen. He was too angry, too saturated in his own sorrow and guilt, the guilt he felt for not doing more to save his family.

'Right now you must learn to be a sailor.' Bugatti went on, clearly unaware or unaffected by James's obvious lack of enthusiasm for the subject. 'BUT FIRST YOU WILL NEED TO BUILD A BIGGER BOAT'. Suddenly his voice had risen sharply and he had lunged straight towards the boy's head with his old hands. The sudden movement startled him but the boy held on even tighter, expecting another forceful push. This time however, he wasn't trying to push him to the ground. His fingers were spread out wide and his palms were rushing towards the side of the boy's head. The very moment that James felt the hands wrap around his temples he was gone.

It was the most peculiar sensation; he couldn't tell if he had lifted up out of his body or fallen deep inside it, everything was happening so fast. The terrain was rushing beneath him at such a pace that it was impossible for him to make sense of it. In the centre of the great blurry mass of land he could make out a thin blue line. He was so high that it took him a while to work out that the line, which twisted and turned its way through the centre of his vision, was in fact the course of a river. Its turns were moving so fast that it literally looked like a snake slithering its way through the landscape. And then suddenly the full force of a wave hit him square in the face. Its icy touch was so severe that for the briefest of moments it felt as if it had burnt him. It had hit him with such a force that it nearly ripped his fingers from the pole he was holding. He experienced a moment of complete terror and confusion, totally unable to make sense of what was happening. As he looked up another wave battered him again but still he held on. The ground beneath him was rocking up and down violently and he looked up again, shivering and scared, he desperately wanted to try and make sense of his surroundings. Straight in front of him stood the man who only moments ago he had watched slide the huge pole of wood into the hard ground as if it was nothing. His long grey beard and hair were soaked through with the cold, wet waves that continued to strike them but his shining eyes brought him a little comfort. James quickly stole a glance around him in the brief gap before the next wave hit. He looked out across the angry, black mass of water that seemed to stretch out infinitely before him. It was as dark as he had ever known it. The only light came from a high, waning moon and a small lantern strapped to the pole far above him, somehow struggling to stay alight. This was it, this was the sea. He looked out at it and he shivered. He shivered at the sheer primordial power of it, at the vastness of it and at the fury of it.

"HOLD ON!", Bugatti shouted but the screaming wind and roaring waves tried to smother the sound as it left his mouth. "Hold on for your life. If the sea claims you then you will be lost out here forever.".

James held on as tightly as he could as yet another freezing wave slapped against him. His hands were numb and the wind was whipping against his cold skin. "Look around you James, this is your ship and this is your sea.". He turned his head to the right and looked out across the wet deck of a boat. The wooden boat stretched out before him. It was crudely built but tough. It fought hard to ride the waves and stay afloat in the waters that seemed to be trying so hard to sink it. Above him the sails buckled and squeaked and flapped under the force of the wind that was assaulting them. The ship was of no great size; it was no match for the huge waves and the vast unrelenting fury of the water that battered it. Suddenly a huge wave hit them and his numb hands almost lost their grip. Only his right hand was still holding the mast but he quickly pulled himself back to the post. Bugatti gave him a worried glance but made no effort to hold him, his eyes told him all that he needed to know; this was his boat, this was his sea and this was his battle. He looked to his left and was suddenly hit with yet another wave but this time it was a sudden wave of shock for it was the first time he had realised that they were not alone. In the blackness beyond he could make out the outline of a small figure clinging to a large round wheel. The figure didn't seem to notice them or if it did then it was too busy bravely fighting against the fury of the storm, battling to steer the boat through these troubled waters. He stared into the blackness of the night desperately trying to make out the figure on whom both their lives depended. He screamed out but whoever it was steering the ship couldn't hear them. Maybe it was just the loud wind stealing his cries. Then he saw. He saw who that little brave figure was and the shock of it almost made him loose his grip again. The figure was so familiar and yet so completely alien to him. Although he had grown up with him his whole life he had never seen him from this angle, he had never had the chance to look at this figure objectively, only from the angle of a mirror, for the brave sailor was himself. It was he who was fighting with the wheel, battling with the winds and trying to keep his little vessel afloat against all the insurmountable odds that faced him. The site of it made him want to weep, to call out to the poor, lonely young boy and to let him know that he wasn't alone but Bugatti drew his attention back.

'This is your sea, this is the sea of emotion, only you can quieten this storm. Your anger and your sorrow will keep battering you until they sink you.' There was a huge snapping noise above them as one of the sails broke from its holding and was now whipping freely through the air. 'Your boat isn't strong enough to withstand all this for long, it's falling apart. You must bring an end to this, quieten your mind, find the eye of the storm.'

'I don't know what you mean', screamed the boy, he was getting frantic now. 'No more riddles, just tell me what to do'.

'Let go of your feelings, do not let them overwhelm you', Bugatti shouted back. 'Let them pass through you.'

James tried but he was just so scared. The blackness of the sea was terrifying and the storm was too great. Another wave hit the ship hard and once again he looked over at the brave boy to his left struggling to keep his grip at the helm. It was too much for him to take and he wept. The final wave hit him straight in the face and he felt himself falling back. His hands had lost their grip, they were too numb and his body too weak to withstand the constant battering. Bugatti's hands darted out in an instant and grabbed him roughly by the arms, pulling him back to the mast.

'We must go, it's too much for you, I'm taking you back.'

'No!', screamed James through the biting wind, 'we can't leave him here on his own, we need to help him'.

'It's only you who can help him James and right now you are making things worse, we must leave.' With that Bugatti reached out and placed his hands on either side of James's wet head and then he fell.

The earth hit the back of his head hard as it smacked against the ground and he was shivering as he came to. The warmth of the fire against his skin was the greatest luxury he had ever felt but even so it took a long time for its heat to warm his bones. Dowser had moved to his side and was licking his cheek as if trying to revive him, to bring him back to this reality which brought with it it's own set of unvanquished fears and sorrows His head was pounding, partly with the impact from the ground and partly because his brain was working so hard to correlate the experience into something he could understand, something he could explain. Fresh tears fell from his tired eyes as he thought of the boy they had left behind, so completely alone and still battling that violent storm.

'The sea of emotion flows inside us all, the waters reach out all the way to the shores of our death'. James was too tired to respond but he had the feeling that Bugatti just wanted him to listen anyway. The man's words were always slow, measured as if each one had been through a rigorous selection process before they passed his lips. Of the many possible combinations of words that could form a sentence James felt as if each of his were constructed with the one perfect fit, perfectly portraying all that he meant even if the meaning escaped the understanding of others.

'It is this vast sea that brings you your joy, your hope, your love and yet it is the same waters which now threaten to drown you in grief, sorrow and hatred. These waters are all you will ever know, their currents are the currents of your whole life.'. Bugatti gazed at the fire as he spoke, seemingly captivated by the dance of the flames in the wind and the sporadic spraying sparks which popped from the burning logs. 'You will experience a great many things out at sea and these things will influence every aspect of your life and your being and the choices you make. How we traverse these waters ultimately decides the quality of both our lives and our deaths. In our final moments they will either comfort us in the warm waters of satisfaction, love and fulfilment or torment us in the icy pinch of sorrow and regret. It is your depth of feeling that brings with it depth of experience but it is your ability to ride the deep waves of these feelings that will determine the quality of your life.' James's eyes had fallen shut, he was exhausted from the experiences of the last couple of days but he listened on quietly, letting the sound of Bugatti's voice soothe him and the words flow through him. 'You must always remember that you can make your own weather, ultimately we are all responsible for making our own weather'.

'In order to cross any great ocean you must first build a boat capable of sustaining such a voyage. The boat must be large and strong. It must be carefully constructed of the finest, materials and painstakingly examined for any cracks or gaps. Every crack must be filled, every seal must be tight and each join scrutinised, for the smallest hole will sink the most sturdy of ships if left unplugged. You are the ship James and it is you.'. James could feel his mind beginning to relax, it felt much like any other overworked muscle, heavy and tired but the words were acting like a sedative or a painkiller as they carried him away from his own thoughts.

'Your ship will grow with you, as you grow. It does not grow in relation to your size or your strength for it is not physical strength that guides you through the waters of the heart. It grows as you learn to truly know yourself, to love yourself; it grows upon the foundations of peace, contentment, love and acceptance that you construct within your own heart. It is self-knowledge, contentment and gratitude that provide the timber and it is love that holds it all together, that fills the cracks and prevents the sea from ever claiming you.... Acceptance" Bugatti seemed to drift of briefly, as if his mind had wandered far from here, far from the fire and the woods and then he went on, his voice was quiet now, little more than a whisper. 'It's our acceptance, our faith in the universe and fate that prevents the waves from ever getting too high, from ever sinking us. Ride that sea, my boy, ride it and marvel at its great many wonders. You will always have storms to contend with, winds will try to rip your sails and waves will crash against your bows but with a strong boat you will be able to ride the waves, to sit safely above the waters that rage beneath you. A quiet mind will help you ride through to the calm waters that always await, where the winds are gentle and warm. To the moment when the sun breaks through the thick cloud for the first time and caresses your skin and fills your heart with joy and gratitude. Build your ship well and there will be no storm too great and no waves too fierce, you will be able to ride this great sea of emotion all the way to your death and beyond.'. His words stopped for he could hear the breaths of the young boy slow and deepen beside him and he smiled as he looked to see his young little friend sleeping peacefully next to him.

20.

James had never been this far from the village before and he was amazed by how different the landscape had become. Over the past few days he had seen so many new things for the first time. He had passed through his first ever rock walled valley, the steep grassy rock-face climbed high into the sky and he almost felt enveloped by the earth. The flowers were different too. Every now and then one would catch his eye and he would think to himself how he must remember to pick some for his mother on the way back. When he thought of his mum, part of him wanted to turn around and head straight back to the village to be with her and to comfort her but another part felt even more determined to return with Julie seated safely with him on Meg's back. He was, however, running out of hope for his little sister. Every hour that passed seemed to chip away at the last little vestiges of hope he still possessed. He had no idea where they were, he was completely lost and he couldn't even confide in Bugatti. He had become used to the spectral sight of the old man sat riding beside him. It was as if he had become air but a dense, transparent air. The light seemed to pass straight through him. There had been a lot of time for thinking over the past few days and James had thought more than he had in the whole of his life. Bugatti had warned him about the dangers of thinking too much. He had described the mind as a wild stallion that need to be tamed, to be called on when needed and set aside when not, but James's thoughts had been galloping through his mind ever since they had set off. His thoughts would often wander to the sphere. What was it? What did it do? He could feel himself longing to be reunited with it and he hated himself for it. The sphere shouldn't matter after everything else he'd been through yet somehow it did. He had even found himself wondering if the hollowness he felt inside was, in fact, the space where the sphere used to be, not where his heart was. Every time he had tried to get answers from Bugatti he had been vague and offered little. He had grown accustomed to his aloofness by now but he seemed to be particularly vague about the sphere, even by his own standards. He had said that the sphere possessed the power of the earth and the stars and of that which created the earth and the stars. That it was the great gift from the earth, greater than a thousand Wayli flowers. This didn't help at all for James knew nothing of those beautiful flowers either! He had said that the sphere gave you the power to become the person you needed to be, to reach the full potential of your birthright. That didn't sound too exciting to him. He just thought of the strange surge of energy that would run through his body every time he touched it and the fascinating, hypnotic colours which danced inside it. He couldn't bear the thought of it being held in the festering hands of those snatchers, it was his - it belonged in his caring, loving hand, not their cruel ones. He wondered why this gift of the earth had been bestowed on him. He wasn't special; there was nothing out of the ordinary about him. He was just a simple boy with a simple village life. What had he done to deserve such a gift, or such a burden as Bugatti so often referred to it.

'This is hopeless', said the young boy. He knew he'd get no reply from Bugatti or Dowser but it was as if he simply needed to hear the sound of his abject despair vocalised. He could feel the rough waters of the sea of emotion churning inside him and he thought of the poor boy who would be struggling to ride their waves. He shivered at the strange memory and tried hard to calm himself for the sake of the young sailor. He rode on but his mind was fighting, he was near to giving up and going back. He had almost resigned himself to the fact that he would never see his sister again. It was only the strange old man's belief in him that kept him moving forwards or backwards or whichever way it was that he was going, that crazy belief that somehow he was leading them the right way. He hated the thought of letting him down, of letting that funny, shaggy-haired dog down so he just continued to ride. The man had told him that he would simply know when to stop and know where to go and that he should listen to his heart, quieten his mind and follow the call of the sphere. He had said that the fact they had taken his sister was actually of great advantage to them. It meant that he had the love of his sister to guide him too, but it certainly didn't feel like it from where he sat.

They were riding through long wild grass with fields that seemed to stretch out on either side as far as the eye could see. Behind them in the distance lay the rich, thick forest from which they had come and up ahead the landscape changed dramatically once again. In front of them a steep rocky incline awaited that seemed to spread out for some distance along the horizon.

'There must be a storm coming', thought James, for above the hill and in the distance thick black clouds were covering the sky. He'd never seen clouds quite like it; they seemed so dense that he imagined they must fill the entire gap between the earth and the stars. A sudden shiver came over him as he looked out at them, there was something sinister and foreboding about them. They didn't seem to move as other clouds he had seen but then again perhaps he was just too far away to see clearly. They started to make their way up the steep rocky cliff. Meg's old hooves struggled to get a grip on the earth and she would sometime slide on the rubble beneath them. Dowser's steps were far less cautious, his comparatively little feet were far more suited to the terrain. It was a long hard climb and Meg was clearly worn out, struggling for breath when they reached the top. She stepped up over the lip and onto the ground above. In front of them the ground was barren and flat, covered with short grass with barely any wild flowers to splash colour on the plain, green canvas. James looked on into the distance and a strange fear gripped him. Ahead the black sky loomed over a dark forest. Dark wasn't the right word though, he just couldn't think of a better adjective to properly explain what he saw, it was as if the clouds had literally drained the sky and land of any colour or light at all. There was something else very disturbing about the distant forest. There were no leaves on any of the trees. The trees almost looked completely dead from this distance. They seemed to stand there as some strange dying monument to the true forest which must have once claimed the land. He rode on slowly, leading them tentatively closer. The atmosphere had completely changed and he could sense Meg's uneasiness. As he got closer he could see that the trees were, in fact, dead. They were black and completely lifeless. In an instant he knew. He remembered back to the horrible dream that had haunted him all those nights ago and he knew exactly where they needed to go.

They were right next to the forest now and every muscle in his body seemed to tighten as if to prevent him from entering. He climbed down from Meg's back. It was mid-afternoon and the sun was warm and bright yet only metres inside the forest it was black as night. He stood as if on the cusp of two totally different worlds. There was no easy path that could lead them through this forest. Bugatti would never be able to make it through on his great horse. He'd never seen Meg like this before, she was snorting and would occasionally rise up on her two old, tired back legs. Her eyes were wide and she was clearly scared herself.

'Bugatti....Bugatti.' There was no reply from the flickering, bearded figure who sat on top of his steed. 'Bugatti, I need you, you have to come back'. James watched as the spectral figure slowly seemed to solidify before his eyes. He was amazed how little it shocked him, he must be becoming accustomed to the great many peculiarities of the man. As Bugatti came to he shook his head and when he opened his eyes it was the first time James had ever seen anything vaguely resembling shock on his regal face.

'We are close James, we are close, I can feel her. We must act quickly, I don't know how much time we have.'. He quickly dismounted his horse and gave him a few hard pats on the side of its long, proud neck. 'Thank you my friend. I may be needing you again soon, please don't go far.'. The horse lifted its head in seeming acknowledgment and turned slowly to walk away from the forest. James grabbed Meg's reins and tried to lead her into the forest but she simply refused. Her feet rooted in the ground and her wide eyes darted from side to side as if searching for the source of her inexplicable fear. James looked around but there was nothing on that flat barren land he could tie Meg to.

'I'm sorry.' He looked into her eyes as he said it, trying to calm the little horse but he was sure she could sense his fear too. 'I'm going to have to tie you to this tree but I promise you will be OK and I will be back for you.' Meg tried to pull away as if she knew what he planned but James tugged her hard and after a short struggle, had managed to tie her.

'Quickly, James, we must go.' As they took their fist steps into the forest and into the cold black night that awaited them only metres from the warm daylight from which they had come, James began to tell Bugatti of his dream. The old man listened intently. James knew where they must go; the dream had been so vivid that he could recall it as if it were a waking memory. None of what they came across was any great shock to him. There was that same eerie silence and total lack of life around them. The sinister sense of malevolence that seemed to fill the whole forest, he'd felt it all before, hw was as prepared as it was possible to be and grateful this time to have someone else by his side. Bugatti could feel Zelda's presence and he was worried that by merely being there he was endangering their chances of retrieving the sphere and saving the little girl from her horrible fate. There was no doubting that his priorities lay in that order. He knew that he must forget himself, indeed stop being himself if he was to keep his presence hidden so he walked on silently trying to empty his mind of all things. He knew that she would be able to find him if she was looking but maybe it could buy him enough time to find somewhere to create another protective circle within which he could hide from her ethereal gaze.

They kept walking further into the heart of the forest and James's instincts told him that they were getting very close now. The dead twigs and wood that littered the forest floor would snap and crack under each hasty step. The noises echoed in the utter silence of the forest and they sounded like small bones breaking underfoot. It was as dark as he had remembered and his heart beat fast in terror at the sight of the tree that he knew lay only slightly further ahead. Bugatti looked up at the tall dead trees, desperately trying to free his mind of thoughts but the rhyme was hard to silence. He had carried it with him for hundreds of years and only now had life been breathed into those words.

> Where trees conceal and waters meet,
> The one shall bring you what you seek.
> Where dead wood trees to heavens reach,
> Shall be the place where two worlds meet
>
> Where day breaks to darkest night,
> Evil feeds like a parasite
> Where children bleed beneath the tree,
> The kingdom of the damned shall be

James stopped them and told Bugatti of what lay ahead. He had listened to the whole of James's dream and knew that somehow the tree would lead down to Zelda, the snatchers and the sphere. He could not be sure if Julie was still alive but if she were then she too would be there. As they walked on it felt almost as if the trees were closing in on them, tightening around them. It was so dark now that they had to walk with their hands stretched out before them to prevent any of the sharp, dry branches from scratching their faces and eyes. James had to strain to see only a few metres in front of him and his heart was beating so hard that he could feel it hitting the inside of his ribcage. In every shadow he thought of the snatchers, waiting to tear at him with their clawed hands and rip the flesh from his bones like they had done with his father. Eventually, after what probably seemed far longer than it actually was, they reached a clearing but the sight that confronted them was more terrifying than the rest of the journey put together. Even though he had seen it before, in reality the tree was far worse than his dream could ever make it. Bugatti suddenly tugged him by the arm and James jumped at the shock of it, he fought to keep the scream from leaving his mouth. Bugatti quickly pulled him back into the thick of the forest from which they had come without uttering a word. There was a ripping sound and James realised it was the noise of the old man tearing the white cloth of one of the many layers of garments that covered his chest. He tied the white cloth to the nearest branch that hung close to his face. He continued to walk back into the forest, marking each tree in the same way every ten metres or so until he had marked about 12 of them. Then Bugatti bent down and picked up a stick. He quickly scratched a round circle in the earth that surrounded them and then finally he spoke.

'The tree is as you foresaw it and it is where your fate has led you. I cannot go with you, James, you foresaw this too. You know what must be done.'

'You can come with me, you can do anything.'

'James', said the old man, his eyes were serious and seemed to shine with a certain sadness. 'Somewhere within that tree lies a very powerful and very dangerous sorceress. We are on her ground now. That tree is protected with a very old and very powerful magic. If I was to enter then she would absorb whatever power I still possess and it would only serve to strengthen her, I cannot allow that.'

James shivered at the thought of having to go in on his own., but he knew that he had brought this fate on his sweet, innocent little sister and if she was still alive then he would endure anything to get her back.

'This flask is filled with a drink made from that beautiful flower you brought me, the Wayli flower. Take three big mouthfuls.'

'What is it? What's it do?', he asked.

'The flower is the planet's great gift to the initiated. It gives the gift of life, prolonged life, strength and vigour. I was born a man, just as you, and should have died many, many years ago. It is the nectar of that magic plant which has given us the strength to travel through these past centuries', he said stroking the head of his old friend. 'This is the last Wayli flower I shall find, of this I'm certain, and I know that my time here is reaching its end'. The sadness in his eyes betrayed his strong face. 'The only way in is going to be through the roots in the tree. You foresaw this and it is so.'

James couldn't believe what he was hearing. Nothing scared him more than those black roots wrapping around his body.

'The juice will make you strong. Its power cannot prevent you dying.' Bugatti's words suddenly had a sinister ring to them but he went on. 'It cannot protect you from death itself but it will give you the health and strength and power to live through many things. The roots will not be able to harm you. You must believe that…the roots will not be able to harm you.'

James sat there shaking at the prospect of what he had to do. It was only a deep love that forced him to continue when every part of him just wanted to run, far from this hateful forest. He held the flask in his hands and took three large sips. It tasted incredibly bitter, with the sharpness of a lemon. As it slid down his throat it felt as if a hot fire was consuming him from the inside. Almost instantly he could feel his muscles twitch and strengthen and the bitterness gave way to a sweetness that hung delicately at the back of his throat. When he gave it back there was only a little left.

'You will be alone in there. You will not be strong enough to fight whatever you find and I have no way of helping you. It is your fate that has brought you to this point and it is your fate that will decide from here. She will not be expecting you to enter through the roots of the tree and she certainly wouldn't expect you to survive if you did. The element of surprise is the only weapon you may wield, so wield it wisely. I do not know what awaits you my little friend.' The old man looked at the boy and the sorrow he felt was etched all over his old, weathered face. 'But I do know that you have been chosen for a reason, that there is a strength within you of which you're still so unaware. There are times in our lives when we must all confront our fate head on and that time for you is now. You must reclaim the sphere. I will be waiting here for your return. Follow the cloth hanging from the tree and I will be waiting. You must get the sphere', he repeated., 'above all things, it is of the greatest importance.' He lifted the flask to his bearded lips and took a few sips of the juice himself, then he poured what little was left into Dowser's mouth. He savoured that sharp nectar as he knew that it would be his last. 'Now my brave little friend, you must go.' Bugatti looked deep in his eyes one last time and James could see a deep sorrow. 'Forgive me, James', he said., 'your fate is greater than I can control.' And with that strange farewell James walked out bravely towards the bloodied soil to offer himself to the tree.

21.

As he stood there in the darkness, cold, alone and afraid, James couldn't work out if the fact that he already knew what was coming brought him any comfort or made things worse. The ground was soft and still a little sticky underfoot from all the blood that had previously been spilt beneath him. He prayed that the blood wasn't that of his own little sister but the little he could see brought him some hope because the blood didn't seem to be fresh, it certainly didn't smell it anyway. He almost didn't dare look up at the enormous tree that towered up above him like some great malevolent force but he didn't want to show the fear that he felt, it was after all just a tree, that's what he had to keep reminding himself. He looked over at the base of it and he could see a small crack in the wood at the bottom, it looked like an opening of some sort. There were fresh markings in the ground where it appeared as if something had been dragged straight through the crack and into the tree itself. He arched his neck backwards to try and look all the way up to the top of the tree but it was too tall. He wondered how much of it had been lost in the darkness, perhaps it reached all the way up the thick clouds which he had seen hanging motionless in the sky. He was scared, petrified, but he was also incredibly angry. The anger seemed to provide him with a little extra strength. He had resolved in his own mind that he was willing to die for his sister, he would give his own life freely if it would prevent her from suffering the same fate he was about to endure. It was after all his fault that she had been taken, it was his fault that the snatchers had sought out his family, destroyed his home and killed his father. As he stood there he felt a strange mix of emotions and a sudden flash of anger and resentment for the old man who had left him here alone in the perpetual night. If he hadn't met the man and his dog then none of this would ever have happened; he would be at home with his sister and his dad in the village without a care in the world and now, after everything, he was being made to face this tree and those creatures and that evil sorceress the old man had spoken of on his own. He was just a boy, wasn't half as strong as the man and definitely couldn't perform any magic. 'Oh well', he thought. There is a strange kind of peace that overcomes someone when they completely surrender themselves to their fate and an incredible strength when they have already decided that they will freely give their life if that is what it takes,. James was feeling both of them. Almost at the very moment he was considering whether or not to approach the entrance at the base of the tree he felt the sudden grip on his ankle. A root had silently lifted up out of the earth and in just a fraction of a second it had clasped him tightly. His whole body jumped with the shock and his heart leapt into his mouth. It was beating hard and fast with the sudden shot of adrenalin that was now coursing through his veins. He decided not to fight it, he would stand there as bravely as he could and he would accept the fate that awaited him. He looked straight up at the menacing tree and felt a courage he didn't know he possessed.

'The roots cannot harm me, you cannot harm me.' He kept repeating the mantra in his mind and he tried desperately hard to believe it. Another root gripped his other ankle, their hold was tight, painfully tight, but still he didn't struggle. They were slowing working their way up his legs now, coiling their way around him like some demonic snake. He gritted his teeth with determination and tried not to think of all the other poor children who had been here before him. They would not take his blood, he would not satisfy their cruel hunger. 'The roots cannot harm me, you cannot harm me.' He didn't once look down at the roots, even when he felt them reach up beyond his waist. He just kept looking up at the tree repeating the words in his mind.

Bugatti sat cross-legged in the centre of the protective circle he had constructed and Dowser lay with his head in the old man's lap. His fingers passed though the dogs hair as he thought of his brave little friend walking to meet his fate. He hated himself for letting the boy go alone and he cursed the forces that had led them both to this point. It had been many, many years since he had spent so much time with anyone and he had quietly developed a deep affection for the boy. A magicians life was a solitary existence and the boy's presence had reminded him of all that he had sacrificed. The guilt he was feeling weighed down heavily on his broad shoulders. He sat there quietly trying to send James all the strength and courage that he could because he knew for sure that the he was going to need it.

The roots were now up to his stomach, trying to crush him and break him but James felt strong. His body felt somehow denser than before and his bones refused to crack under the force of those roots. As the roots snaked up towards his chest he took one last long, deep breath. They were trying to crush his lungs and force all the air out of him but he fought with every bit of strength he possessed to hold that breath inside him.

Bugatti turned to look at the boy who stood there so bravely. The blackness was all-consuming but his powerful, well-trained eyes could just about make out what was happening. He could barely see the roots wrapping their way around his little friend but what he could make out was enough. He had seen a great many things in his long life but this was too much for him, he couldn't watch anymore. He turned his head downwards in shame and a small tear fell from his eye and wet the head of his old friend. Suddenly, in one lightning flash the roots pulled, ripping the boy downwards, deep into the earth below.

22.

James held that last breath as long and hard as he could. The roots squeezed and squeezed, trying to crush and to force the blood from his body into the soil that surrounded him. Their grip was so immense but they couldn't break him. He just kept repeating those words in his head, desperately tensing every muscle in his body, fighting for his life. Now that he was deep in the earth he tried to struggle, to somehow free himself from their vice-like grip. The soil was still loose around him, loose enough to enable him to move but it was heavy and dense making every movement so unbelievably difficult. He was using up the little valuable oxygen that he had left and he could feel his chest get tighter and his lungs begin to burn with their desire for breath. He couldn't breathe because the loose soil was packed against his face and mouth. He fought but their grip was just too tight, he was no match for them and the thought crossed his mind that this was it, he had failed his sister and he too was going to become yet another young corpse left to rot into this poisoned earth. Suddenly however, the roots just let go, loosened their hold on him. It was as if they had given up, had become confused by the fact his bones wouldn't break and that no blood would spill. The weight of the soil was still pinning him down though and making it impossible for him to breathe, he had to hold out still longer. He kept pushing the dirt aside, clawing at it with his bare hands. Climbing higher and higher using the roots as his guide. All their movement had made the earth soft. His head was light and he knew his breath was running out. He kept climbing further, pushing the earth away but each time he cleared a little then more would fall in its place. The Wayli juice had made him strong and he could feel its energy flowing through him but it couldn't keep him alive for too much longer, he desperately needed to reach the top, to reach air. He was growing weaker, his heart was beating so hard to keep him alive. He felt as though his head was going explode and his lungs were screaming for air. Finally he pushed the last piece of soil away and forced his head up into the cavern. He took the biggest breath of that stinking air that he could and still it tasted sweet. He fought to be as quiet as he could but each breath was heavy, deep and desperate.

Zelda stirred in her deep sleep. Her dreams had taken her back to a time which was now long gone, a time she had hoped to forget. To a man she had known in a world far removed from the one she found herself in now, somewhere between the living and the dead. To one of her greatest enemies and to a man she could have loved had the black grip of evil not captured her soul so completely. Her dreams were vivid, they had taken her far from the filthy existence she would awaken to and she wanted them to go on.

James looked into the dark cavern he had found himself in. A few embers still glowed a warm red in the middle of the room. It was hard to make anything out in the shadows but on the opposite side he could just about see the silhouette of something hanging from the earthy roof and what looked like a few crates. He looked everywhere for Julie, scouring every inch of the darkness. As he turned to the right he had to stop himself from squealing in shock. For close to him lay a young lady. Where feet should have been he could see black tree roots that buried into the ground below. He shuddered, knowing instantly that she was the evil which lay at the heart of the tree. He could make out that familiar soft, sparkling glow emanating from her fist and he didn't need to go any closer to know that it was the sphere. His heart was beating so loudly that he worried it would wake her. He could hear her soft breaths as she slept and then froze rigid as she gently stirred. The smell was repulsive. The stench of the snatchers and their rotting carcasses permeated the damp air and it nearly forced him to retch. The woman lay there partly covered with an animal skin but a breast, pale shoulders and arm lay outside. Even from where he was he could see that she was beautiful, captivatingly beautiful. He had never seen a face quite like it, her features were perfect and he had to shake his head to bring himself out of the trance-like gaze he was in. As quietly as possible he pulled himself from the ground. There was no turning back now. When he was completely free he crouched down as close to the cave wall as possible and began to look around on the floor. His eyes had become accustomed to the dark now and the Wayli juice had greatly improved his vision. He searched silently. After a little looking he found a small round stone. It was nowhere near as smooth as the sphere but it would have to do. Slowly and silently he started to make his way towards the sleeping lady.

Julie had heard movement. She sat bolt upright in her cage, ears pricked and eyes desperately searching in the darkness. Across the other side of the room she finally realised what had been making those soft noises. She could see a figure slowly creeping towards the sleeping lady. Her heart leapt with both fear and joy at the same time. It was a person. Not tall enough for a man though, she thought. As the boy moved closer to the lady who lay rooted on the floor Julie got more and more afraid. She was going to wake and then he'd be thrown in the other cage and then they'd have no chance of getting out. She had paid close attention to which tunnel led back up to earth as little more had filled her mind than the thought of crawling back out of here.

'Psssssh', she let out the quietest sound she could and the sneaking figure stopped dead in its tracks.

James stood there as still as a statue but with his heart beating hard in his chest, he was so close to the sleeping lady that he could almost reach out and touch her. He looked down at her and he'd never seen anyone so beautiful. Her beauty matched that of the sphere she was holding. He could have gazed at her all night. With her sleeping eyes closed and her light little breaths it was hard to imagine the evil that must lie within. James was totally transfixed and then there it was, that sound again. He looked over into the dark corner from where it came, careful only to move his neck so as not turn on the dirt beneath him. 'Julie', he thought, 'it must be Julie.' His heart suddenly filled him with a hope he had scarcely let himself feel before. He longed to call out, to find out straight away if it was her but he knew that if he did then they would never make it out of there. He had to be silent, quieter than he had ever been, but he couldn't quieten that thumping heart which bounced within him.

Julie couldn't believe it. As the figure had turned to look, the soft embers had shone the smallest light on his face. It was James, no mistaking it. She had spent many nights talking to that face in the moonlit bedroom at night and it was as familiar to her in the darkness as it was in the clear light of day. She wanted to scream to him so much. She wanted to shout for him to run over and save her but she didn't dare. Pushing her face right up to the bony bars in the hope that there would be enough light for him to see her, she waited.

He searched the darkness. There was a dead animal hanging from the ceiling as well as the crates. His eyes bore through the darkness, searching, hoping. Then he saw her, he was overcome with such a sudden surge of love for her as he saw her little face pushing hard against the bars that held her. A joy captured him, one that almost broke through the grip of fear he was feeling. The snatchers must be close, their stench was so strong. He had to stay strong and brave, he had to save her. It was all down to him, there would be no-one else coming. If he failed then he couldn't even bear to think of what would become of her. Her sad eyes were calling him and he was coming.

He was too close to the lady to go now. He knew that this was his only chance to reclaim the sphere. Seeing it again had made him realise just how much he longed for its touch and he felt that it longed for him too just as much. He edged closer and she stirred again. There was no going back though and nothing else he could do so he fought against his fear and carried on until he was close enough to kneel down beside her. He held his breath so that the noise and the touch of it wouldn't disturb her. He had to keep reminding himself that this was the lady who had put Julie in the cage but even now he found it hard to believe, how could something so beautiful be capable of such atrocities? Her pale hand hung down beneath him and he reached for it. He had the small stone in one hand and with the other he gently reached in for the sphere. Her grip on it was sleepy and soft but as he reached for it she let out a sudden sharp breath and moved slightly in her sleep. He was so frightened that his poor heart couldn't beat any faster. Again he reached in. This time he had it, he managed to slide the small round stone into its place as he did. The electricity tickled his spine and he tried not to shiver. The sphere felt like an old friend and he revelled in its perfect touch. He turned now to head over to Julie but as he did the sleeping woman began to stir. This time though it was clear that she was waking.

He held the sphere tightly in his hand. He couldn't believe how good it felt to have it back. Even now though he noticed something slightly different in the way it felt, something unfamiliar. He made his way as quickly and quietly as he could to Julie, her haunted eyes pleading with him to hurry. After what felt like an eternity he managed to reach the cage door and he softly stroked her little fingers that held so tightly onto the bars. Their scared little eyes met and he knelt down to better look at the cage door. A piece of bone had been wedged in hard to keep the door locked. He pulled at it but still it held. He pulled again and managed to slide it free and the door creaked open. The noise was amplified in the hollow cave, it seemed to bounce all around them and they knew instantly that they would soon be out of time and that the sleeping woman would almost certainly awaken.

Zelda's dream was hard to leave. The man that she had once loved was there with her, calling her. He held out his hand and was asking her to follow him down a beautiful woodland path. His shaggy-haired dog bounced playfully around them and she was filled with emotions she hadn't felt for centuries, emotions she didn't know she possessed anymore. But there was something else calling her, a sense of unease. There was a distant noise coming and she knew she must force herself to wake, drag herself back to the reality that tormented her. She began to pull herself from the dream and as she did she could immediately sense that something wasn't right. It had been a trick, she knew it in an instant, the man had invaded her dreams and had been trying to hold her there, she hated him for it and she hated herself for being taken in by it. She hated herself for once more allowing those pathetic feelings to get the better of her. She would never allow herself to be tricked by love again.

Julie's wet eyes looked out at him with a mixture of absolute terror and unconditional love and gratitude. She was desperately trying to contain the noise of her sobbing but her short sharp breaths cut through that silent damp air like a knife. James reached out his hand and felt her soft fingers on his. As he pulled her towards him he could already hear the whistling breath of the snatchers coming from somewhere in the distant blackness that surrounded them. The thought of seeing their foul features again terrified him but his hatred for them and what they had done gave him strength. He pulled her up by the hand and as she looked at him she pointed down the tunnel that led out to the ground above, to possible salvation. They didn't know yet how they would defeat the snatchers, all they knew is that every fibre in both their bodies wanted to get out of that stinking, dark cave, even if what awaited outside was yet more darkness.

23

Zelda woke with a jolt. She knew instantly that she had been tricked and that the sphere had been taken from her. She looked over to her right and saw the small fair-haired boy pulling the girl from her cage. Her scream tore its way from her lungs and filled every corner of that cavern in an instant. Bouncing down the distant tunnel where the snatchers slept, huddled together in one festering mass. 'GET HIM, Get HIM, GETTTTT HIIMMMMMM……..HE'S GOT THE SPHERE.'

The scream shook through James's body as he pulled Julie from the cage. The voice was full of an almost unearthly hatred and venom.

'This way', Julie said, pulling James across the room.

'GET AFTER THEM', the voice screamed again. 'ARRRRRHHH-HHH!' Her howling shrieks filled the air all around them and snatchers snapped awake in an instant. Julie was running up the tunnel as fast as her little legs could take her. The screams were echoing in the caverns below them and they could hear the scramble of the snatchers behind. They kept running into the darkness and James could see up ahead a slightly lighter shade of black, which he hoped would lead them outside. It wasn't far and he knew that they could make it but the snatchers were gaining, he could hear their hisses getting closer and closer. Finally they reached the crack in the wood and Julie managed to squeeze through easily because she was so small, James was finding it harder. The snatchers were almost on him. His shirt had caught on a sharp wooden crag and his heart was beating so loudly that it echoed in the wooden hollow. With one last push he ripped his shirt away from the dead tree and finally he was outside at last, he almost couldn't believe it.

'Bugatti', he shouted hard with all the air in his lungs but there was no reply. It was still so dark but their eyes had become so accustomed to it they could just about make out the dark, shadowy silhouettes of the trees around them. The first clawed hand of the snatcher had gripped the side of the opening and was squeezing its way out through the crack. He grabbed little Julie's hand and pulled her towards the trees.

'RUN', he screamed as he caught the movement of the roots sliding their way silently towards her. 'Quick, follow the white cloth in the trees.' Julie was crying, wailing with all the fear she had felt for the past few days. She could just about make out the white cloth that James was talking about and together they ran hand in hand, as fast as they could, blindly into the darkness beyond.

The first of the snatchers was out. It's piercing eyes staring wildly out into the black forest. The children were running, all the time chased by the roots which snapped behind them.

'BUGATTI', he screamed again.

Again he shouted his name but still there was no reply. He held Julie's hand and was almost pulling her through the trees now. The snatchers were out, chasing them down through the woods. The children were still a little way ahead but it wouldn't be long until they reached them. James had managed to lead them to the final cloth but looked around in utter disbelief as there was no-one there. The old man had deserted them. He refused to believe it, he couldn't have, he wouldn't have, surely. 'BUGATTI', he screamed again but there was no time. The snatchers' evil eyes were upon them and they were hissing their way through the trees towards them. James reached into his pocket and looked at his sister. He placed the sphere in her hand.

'Take this' he said, wrapping her little hands tightly around it as he did. She looked down briefly at the strange object that glowed softly in her hand but didn't give it much attention, she was too scared and she knew the snatchers were coming. She could hear the sound of the dead wood snapping beneath every stride they took and they were getting closer.

'Run', James urged. 'Keep running that way and never stop, I'll find you...RUN.' He screamed it straight into her face and she turned away, she was so scared, but she did as he said. She gripped the strange object tightly in her hand, fresh tears flowed down her face and she ran into the black woods ahead. James watched as she faded into the darkness and was swallowed by the eternal night.

James turned to face the snatchers, they were so close now but he still had a head start on them. He raised his hand in the air and screamed out towards them 'If this is what you want then come and get it' he cried. The snatchers didn't need any more encouragement, Zelda had made it clear enough,. Get the boy, he had the sphere, he had what she needed. The little one could wait, she wouldn't get far and they would hunt her down soon enough. Let her have this short moment of freedom. Her fear would be amplified by this brief moment of hope when they caught her again.

24

Bugatti sat cross-legged in the centre of the crudely marked circle. His closed eyelids fluttered as he delved deep inside his mind. This time it was he who was searching. He was looking for Zelda, quietly creeping up on her awareness, stalking her. Incredibly to his great fortune he found that she was dreaming. He had to search far and wide to find her attention but their connection was still strong, surprisingly so, and it didn't take long. He began to carefully construct a dream world of his own around him. If he could lure her into his world then he knew that he could hold her there for a little while, she could get lost in his dream-like maze and that would at least buy the boy a little time. He built the labyrinth of woodland and created a beautiful path that led down deep into the maze. There wasn't much time, he could feel her dream beginning to crack and break, he had to hold her here just a little longer. He walked up the wooded path and broke out into her dream beyond. He found her standing in the old stone ruins of the magical temple that had been so familiar to them both. Her dreams clearly fought to bring her back to a time that she must surely have longed to leave behind, he knew only too well that there was nothing but suffering for her here. She turned, instantly feeling his presence as his dream began to blend into hers. As her gaze met his for the first time in all those years it was hard for him not to feel some of the love that they had once both shared. She was as beautiful as he had remembered, possibly even more so, but her eyes,; there was something so different in her eyes. He stared deep into those dark, beautifully haunted eyes, desperately looking for any sign of the Zelda he had once known, the woman he had once loved. If she was shocked then she didn't show it, her poise was impeccable, her demeanour seemingly unaffected. A long white dress hung beautifully from her delicate frame and both the dress and her black hair shimmered gracefully in the breeze. Their eyes were locked, both searching, both fighting. He beckoned her towards him and the silence between them was filled with the thousands of memories that they shared. Her eyes began to grow more sinister, more untrusting and he watched as deep cracks began to appear in the dream world her subconscious had constructed; he was losing her, she was waking. He looked at her again, this time more longingly, his eyes called her over, begging her not to leave him and even he couldn't tell how much of that was illusion. She began to take a couple of steps towards him and he held out his arms, inviting her into his embrace. Then suddenly her world shattered, it was being torn apart, something in the other world had startled her. She took one last look at him but this time her eyes were venomous, they were filled with something unearthly, a look he had never seen before and one he would not wish to again. Then her dream collapsed, the images fell in on themselves and she vanished along with them, disappearing like smoke in the wind.

Bugatti pulled himself back to consciousness. He opened his eyes only to be greeted by the blackness that enveloped him. He had done all he could for James. He hoped that he had bought him just enough time but he knew that he would be finding out either way very soon. He quickly rose to his feet and turned, leaving the safety of the circle. He walked away, hating himself for what he knew he had to do.

He heard it all. He listened as James had screamed helplessly for him. He stood there hiding in the dark and it broke his heart. Every part of his being wanted to run to the boy and his little sister, to scoop them up in his arms and carry them away to safety but his great teacher had told him what must be done when he met the boy who carried the sphere. Their stories had been written long ago and he had been told the part he must play. For there was another rhyme that he had been taught to recite time and time again and the words were no longer a mystery to him.

Where day is night and night is day,
Where the dead still lives in a dark, damp cave.

You lead the one unto their fate,
You lead the one you must betray.

He must choose to sacrifice
Not once, his life, but twice

Don't rid him of the life he gave,
He'll choose to fall to rocky grave

Take the sphere to somewhere safe,
For sixty nights and sixty days

Bugatti wept. He cursed whichever foul force had placed him in this situation but he knew that it was far greater than he. He had watched on as his brave little friend had given Julie the sphere and sent her off into the woods. He watched the helpless child turn and run into the woodland with the snatchers chasing him in hot pursuit. Bugatti looked away. His eyes were wet with guilt and sorrow. He turned to run after Julie with Dowser as always by his side.

20.

It had worked. They had left Julie to run into the woods and all three of them were chasing hard after the carrier. His hand was outstretched before him pushing the dead branches aside. But as he ran from the snatchers that followed, thorns and branches still tore at his skin. He could feel blood slowly trickling down his face but he knew he mustn't stop. As soon as they realised he no longer had the sphere then their keen eyes would quickly hunt Julie down in the black forest. He ran onwards through the dense dark trees as fast as he could. The Wayli juice had given him strength and a super-human speed that the snatchers could only just match. He could hear the sound of them smashing relentlessly through the trees and the sound of their feet getting closer. Eventually the forest began to get less and less dense and he could begin to make out sunlight at the very edge of the wood. He ran on, faster than he had ever run in his life, desperate to make it all the way to the light, to be rid of this dark, cold wood. The snatchers were so close to him now that he could hear the hissing of their breath but he was now only metres away from the edge, from the light. As he burst through the final tree his heart nearly stopped. He had to suddenly, slide to an abrupt halt as he found himself teetering on the cliff edge of a vast deep canyon. The sunlight was so close that he could almost reach out to it but there was no further he could go, he was a prisoner to the cold, eternal night. He looked down and saw the sunlight shining on the boulders and rocks that lay so far below.

The snatchers approached him slowly. They couldn't risk the sphere falling down with the boy into the canyon. He turned slowly to face them; their foul, long faces glared at him and they hissed menacingly through their sharp teeth. He looked deep into their cold, dead eyes and he didn't fear them, he simply hated them. He thought of Julie running through the woods and he knew that every second he could buy her would give her the chance to find little, old Meg who could lead her home. He thought of his father who had fought so bravely against these fearsome monsters. He knew that they could rip him to pieces and he wasn't going to give them the chance. His hand was held high above his head in a tight fist. The snatchers were trying to circle him, to force him away from the edge but he just stood there. Then slowly he brought his hand down in front of him as if to offer it out to them. They scrutinised his every move and glanced at each other as if trying to decide what to do. James just remained, rooted to the spot with arm held out. 'Come on then take it, what are you waiting for?' he screamed. "Take it.' The snatchers took the bait. Two of them greedily reached out for his hand. As they did he opened his fist and grabbed them. They saw in an instant that his hand was empty and that they had been deceived. They realised then that he no longer had the sphere and they hissed in disgust at the young boy. He held on to them as tight as he could and watched as the third snatcher turned without a thought and ran straight back into the woodland on its desperate search for Julie. He thought of his little sister running through the forest and he hoped and prayed that she would be reaching the edge. The thought of her filled him with as much strength as the Wayli juice did. The two snatchers fought desperately to free themselves and to join the hunt but still he held on tight. They tore at his skin with the razor sharp talons on their two free hands, scratching at him, snarling, trying to claw themselves free but still he held on. He pulled with all his strength. The juice had made him strong and gradually he managed to pull them closer to the edge. Blood was flowing down his arm and the warm liquid almost made him loose his grip but he kept on pulling. The snatchers dug their feet into the ground but somehow he was pulling them closer and closer, they tried to pull back but he was fighting with everything that he had, fuelled by a deep love and Wayli juice. His feet were balanced on the edge of the cliff now. The snatchers slashed out again and tore deep lines of flesh from his chest. But every time they clawed he managed to lean just a little bit further over the edge. His grip was strong and try as they may to break free he was never going to let go. His eyes burnt with absolute determination and love for his little sister. The snatchers feet were skidding slowly closer to edge. The weight of gravity was pulling him down further and further. He looked straight into their cold eyes and saw that they were afraid and that was all he needed to give him the strength for the one last great tug. He took a deep breath, his head was feeling light from all the blood that he had lost and he was beginning to feel his strength deserting him. Then he gave that one last pull, gravity did the rest and together they began to fall. He looked deep into the foul creatures terrified eyes and he felt the satisfaction of avenging his father. As the sunlight hit them he watched as they began to disintegrate in front of his eyes. He would love to have watched them crash into the rocks below but then he realised that if Julie could just reach the edge of the forest, reach the sunlight then she would be safe. He wished that he could have taken all three of them with him but he knew that he had done all he could.

As he fell he felt the moment his body passed through the shadows and into the sunlight. Even in the rushing wind he could feel the warm rays touch his skin. He closed his eyes and felt his blood warm. He didn't scream as he fell, he didn't even think of the rocks that were rushing up to meet him, instead he journeyed deep inside himself, deep into the waters of his body. He flowed down the brooks until they joined the river and he followed the river which led still deeper and deeper inside. He made sure to pay close attention to all the wonders he passed along the way. He savoured these last beautiful moments because the river was widening and ahead it led out into a beautiful, calm sea. He could make out the outline of a boat on the horizon and he knew that he was home. He let the river carry him into the sea and took one last satisfied breath before he was swallowed by the fifth element which lay both within and without of this body he had known.

25.

Bugatti had soon caught up with the sobbing, scared child. 'Julie', he called but not so loud so as to attract attention. 'Julie.' She slowed down and turned to face him. Her young eyes had seen so much horror in the past few hours that to her, even the old man's fierce face seemed soft and loving. He knelt down and she rushed straight into his arms. He held her tenderly. She pressed her little face deep into his chest and cried.

'We must keep moving', he said softly but forcefully.

'But James, I've got to wait for James…..he said he'd come and find me.' Her small voice shook.

'James has fought to save your life and now it is up to us to make sure he didn't fight in vain.' He smiled at the little girl, his eyes shone with the love she'd seen so often in her father's.

'He gave me this', she said, reaching out with a trembling hand. Bugatti wrapped his two large hands around hers. He couldn't understand. He thought the carrier had to live and die with it in his hands. Well James's blood ran through Julie's veins, he just hoped that would be enough. He squeezed her little hands between his own and said, 'you hold on to that for a little bit longer. Think of it as a little part of your brother, as all the best parts of your brother, and we shall carry him safely away with us'.

Bugatti took her by the hand and led her out from the woods to where Meg waited. Julie was so pleased to see Meg, she ran over and placed her hands on the sweet little old horse and all those memories of home came rushing back to her. Bugatti picked her up and lifted her onto Meg's back. He untied the little mare and took her by the reins. Julie was still sobbing as he led them both out into the flat lands that lay safely away from that terrifying forest.

As he led them away his keen ears were still listening out for any sounds coming from the silent forest. The sounds were so faint that no normal man could have heard them but then Bugatti was no normal man. He could hear the snatchers hiss in terror as they fell through the air. He could hear the wind whistling past their bodies and then he heard the one solitary thud of a body crashing into the earth below. He turned to look out at the evening sunlight that was already beginning to turn a deep, rich red. He watched its light bathe the grassy plains beneath them and his clear eyes filled with tears. He hid his tears from the little girl but he knew that he would never be able to forgive himself for the part he had played in his young friend's death, even if it had been preordained. He cried for the little boy's lost youth and for all that might have been. He had walked the Earth for so many years and there were still so many questions he couldn't answer. Yet as terrible and unkind as this life could be the warm sunlight flooding the plains reminded him that it was equally beautiful and wonderful.

He looked up at the little girl who sat clutching the sphere on the old horse and he knew that this journey had only just begun. He looked into her sad, gentle eyes and it reminded him of all the goodness that humankind can possess, all the potential. He had seen a great many things and perhaps this one little but very important fact had been lost on him over time. As he led the horse by the reins he found himself thinking, 'I suppose maybe I could have just one apprentice', and in the earth beneath his feet and the sky above and all that stretched out before him he felt his master's smile and Bugatti smiled back.

Printed in Great Britain
by Amazon